THE BUCKSKIN HILLS

Lauran Paine who, under his own name and various pseudonyms has written over 900 books, was born in Duluth, Minnesota. His family moved to California when he was at an early age and his apprenticeship as a Western writer came about through the years he spent in the livestock trade, rodeos, and even motion pictures—where he served as an extra because of his expert horsemanship in several films starring movie cowboy Johnny Mack Brown. In the late 1930s, Paine trapped wild horses in northern Arizona and, for a time, worked as a professional farrier. Paine came to know the old West through the eyes of many who had been born in the previous century and he learned that Western life had been very different from the way it was portrayed on the screen. "I knew men who had killed other men," he later recalled. "But they were the exceptions. Prior to and during the Depression, people were just too busy eking out an existence to indulge in Saturday-night brawls." He served in the U.S. Navy in the Second World War and began writing for Western pulp magazines following his discharge. It is interesting to note that all of his earliest novels (written under his own name and the pseudonym Mark Carrel) were published in the British market and he soon had as strong a following in that country as in the United States. Paine's Western fiction is characterized by strong plots, authenticity, an apparently effortless ability to construct situation and character, and a preference for building his stories upon a solid foundation of historical fact. *Adobe Empire* (1956), one of his best novels, is a fictionalized account of the last twenty years in the life of trader William Bent and, in an off-trail way, has a melancholy, bittersweet texture that is not easily forgotten. In later novels like *The White Bird* (1997) and *Cache Cañon* (1998), he showed that the special magic and power of his stories and characters had only matured along with his basic themes of changing times, changing attitudes, learning from experience, respecting Nature, and the yearning for a simpler, more moderate way of life. The film *Open Range* (Buena Vista, 2003), based on Paine's 1990 novel, starring Robert Duvall, Kevin Costner, and Annette Bening became an international success.

THE BUCKSKIN HILLS

Lauran Paine

GUNSMOKE

This hardback edition 2009
by BBC Audiobooks Ltd
by arrangement with
Golden West Literary Agency

ISBN 978 1 405 68244 2

British Library Cataloguing in Publication Data available.

Printed and bound in Great Britain by
CPI Antony Rowe, Chippenham, Wiltshire

CHAPTER ONE

THEY LAY in velvet folds, barren except for tan grass, off in the soft distance, roll after roll of them to break the monotony of an otherwise flat landscape. The Buckskin Hills.

To a stranger's first view they seemed crumpled in disarray, cast down like that in ages gone by a giant hand which had afterwards swept them nude. Beyond the sun in their secret clefts there *were* trees, oaks; even some cottonwoods with their pale bark and two-toned leaves, but only where the springs lay among their thrusts and rises, and unless a person rode to each hilltop and gazed downward, he'd pass by those secret places.

In winter they were invitingly treacherous, their earth slippery, their heights wind-scourged. In summertime they baked and shimmered, their grasses cured on the stem, their folds hidden in an almost perpetual gloominess. But in the springtime there was no place like the Buckskin Hills. At least the people who lived among them, ran their cattle over a thousand knolls and knew every waterhole, felt that way. Which was why Arnold Holfinger sat in the coolness of Annakin's *Blue Mule Saloon* in the town of Bullhead out on the westerly plain, sipping cold beer and studying the thin-face and grey-eyes across the table from him.

Holfinger was new to the Buckskin Hills. That is, he'd come to the Bullhead country the year previous, and almost at once had run into trouble. Not particularly because the people who lived back in there were any more troublesome than people anywhere, but because Arnold Holfinger had brought three thousand Texas cattle with him, and seven Texas rangeriders. He had turned his cattle loose in the Buckskin Hills where they'd over-grazed like locusts, eating everything in sight, and during the fierce mid-summer, his men had come upon a dead steer with a message spelt out on its hide in blood.

'Take your cattle and get out.'

That was all. Just that one shot-steer and that one warning. That had been the year before. Now, Holfinger's seven Texans had a new camp. It was atop a hill instead down in the swale where the spring was. It made them irritable to have to fetch water to the top and to go down there to fetch in the saddle animals every morning. It also made them irritable because the people back in the hills rode by them in Bullhead without glancing their way, and when they met them on the range they were as cold as ice.

The man sitting across from Holfinger threw back his head, drained off his beer, and set the glass down with hard finality. "What do you want me to do?" he asked. "One dead steer's not enough cause to raise much hell."

"I want you," stated Arnold Holfinger quietly, "to do what stock detectives are supposed to do. Ride through those damned hills; keep out of sight. See which ones are their leaders, spy on all of them. Get friendly with them if you can." Holfinger leaned forward. "Because they're going to make trouble and on open range like that nobody—nobody—makes trouble for me. If they try it I want to know in advance. They warned me last year. This year it's my turn."

Holfinger pushed his half-empty glass aside and watched the other man stand up. He made quite a sight. He was tall and lean and had a look of granite toughness about him. His face was weathered and scorched a dark shade of brown, like saddle-leather. He was a loner; a man who spent his time apart from other people. The way he wore his belt-gun said plainly he knew what it was there for.

Holfinger smiled upwards. "Brent, I think you're exactly what I need out here. The more I see of you the more I feel things will work out just right."

Brent's eyes turned veiled and ironic. "The pay," he murmured. "You've talked all around it, Mister Holfinger. If things work out it'll only be because you haven't neglected that one thing—the pay."

Holfinger's smile faded. He reached for the beer glass and toyed with it. "What's the going rate?" he softly asked.

"Depends, Mister Holfinger, on what their leaders are worth to you—dead. And what burnin' them out is worth to you."

Holfinger went right on twisting the beer glass forth and back. His expression did not change. Neither did the subdued brightness of his hard blue eyes. He said, "Brent, you're my man. I never mentioned killin' or burnin'. You did."

Brent leaned and put both hands atop the table. "Mister Holfinger," he said, "folks don't send for me to christen their babies. If you don't want my services all you got to do is say so. Otherwise, Mister Holfinger, it'll cost you two hunnert for each killin' and one hundred for each fire."

"How'll you know which ones are needing your attention?"

Brent hung there gazing at Holfinger, then he hauled up and straightened up off the table. "I'll know," he said. "It may take me a week or more to find out, but I'll know. An' I won't be ridin' back to Bullhead to hunt you up each time. You either trust me or you don't."

Holfinger shoved the glass away from him. He lifted his rugged features to Brent. "Like I said, Brent, the more I see of you the more I'm convinced you're exactly what I need out here. All right; you've set the prices. I'll pay them. Contact me when you can. I live in the hotel down the road. Just remember one thing; if you get into serious trouble I don't know you."

Brent nodded. "That the way the game is played, Mister Holfinger. You don't know me, I don't know you—and you don't do no talkin' in front of your Texas riders or anyone else. Agreed?"

"Agreed," said Holfinger, and turned his head to watch the stock detective leave the saloon. "Agreed. Hey, Joe, bring me something stronger. This beer is what we wean babies on down in Texas."

The barman grinned and became instantly alive. "Right away, Mister Holfinger."

Bullhead creaked and groaned slightly as a pleasant springtime breeze came down from the north carrying the scent of lupin and nopal in bloom. It was a utilitarian town set athwart a broad stageroad running almost due north and south. It had corrals east of town and a little fresh-water creek to the west. It had been that water, precious in Arizona, which had prompted the original founders to start their town out in the middle of the prairie instead of up closer to the Buckskin Hills, or even northward, where some genuine mountains loomed blue-hazed in the spring sunshine.

But the founders had moved on, the rangemen had arrived in Bullhead Basin, and what had once been an outpost of empire became cattle country. Or, to put it another way and using the words of rickety old Sam Stubbs, a country doesn't really come into its own until the settlers get rid of the soldiers.

And Sam should've known. He'd ridden out of the northward Rockies at seventeen years of age with a band of marauding Arapaho on his trail, and that had been a very long time ago. Sam said often and cheerfully that he had no idea how old he was exactly, but his closest calculations led him to believe he'd have to be at least eighty-five, and maybe even actually closer to a hundred and fifty.

Sam Stubbs had a sense of humour. Sometimes it was so droll it wasn't even noticed. Other times it was about as subtle as a falling tree. But he hadn't laughed at many things since Arnold Holfinger'd arrived in the Bullhead country, for Sam's brood lived in a fold of the Buckskin Hills, had lived there ever since Sam had hit the country, and had run their orry-eyed cattle all over that country for the same length of time.

There were others. The newlywed Bronsons, the unmarried Spangler brothers, the Sargents and the Canes, cattle people every one of them, and mostly, second-generation-folk in the Buckskin Hills.

They were resourceful, tough, resilient people. They had to be to make their living running cattle in the southern Arizona country where drought and sandstorm, desert summers and bleak winter-time flashfloods were as normal as sunshine and roses were elsewhere.

Sheriff Holbrook of Apache County told Arnold Holfinger once, that everyone, even the Indians of a generation ago, had been underestimating those hill people to their sorrow for a long time, and if they'd invited Holfinger to leave their hills, it just might not be a bad piece of business to take that advice right seriously.

Holfinger's reply had been short. "In Texas we eat their kind for breakfast ever' morning, Sheriff."

But Tim Holbrook knew the Texas boasts; he'd spent his youth below the Rio Grande too, and if Holfinger wouldn't take the threat seriously, Sheriff Holbrook did. He rode out to the Stubbs place in early spring of the following year, which was when the hill people turned their cattle out, and caught Sam at his home in a broad swale where oaks and cottonwoods made rich shade and a kind of acidy fragrance.

Holbrook was a medium-sized close-coupled man with the power of a kicking mule in each fist and the shrewdness of a lifetime peace officer under his curl-brimmed hat. At forty he'd seen it all, participated in most of it, could scent it coming six months ahead, and always spelt it with a capital T. Trouble.

Old Sam was smoking a pipe on his porch—the Mexicans of that border country called them *ramadas* —when Sheriff Holbrook rode up, got down, tied his horse to a stud-ring in a nearby big cottonwood and walked on up. Old Sam went right on smoking; the only indication his seamed, ancient old rugged face gave that he surmised Tim Holbrook wasn't paying just a social call was in the way his hooded old pale eyes clouded over with a crafty caution.

"Set," he said. "It's good to see you, Tim." Sam removed the pipe, spat lustily into the geranium bed and made a slow, raffish smile. "In fact, it's good to see *anyone*, come spring each year. It's good just to see the springtime again. A feller gets my age he never knows when that consarned trumpet's goin' to blow."

Sheriff Holbrook reached up to tilt back his hat. Around him were the laboriously created barns and buildings it had taken a long lifetime to erect in this woodless country. Sam had three sons, all married. Two lived on the ranch, the third, Dennis, was a lawyer over at Prescott. Rumour had it that Dennis Stubbs would one day run for governor, or at least get the appointment as Territorial Advocate. It was a close-knit clan; even the girls who married into it became dyed-in-the-wool Stubbses after a year or two. The pioneering blood didn't seem to dilute as it had among the other hill people.

"Well, Tim," old Sam said, expectorating again. "Get it off your chest. You didn't ride out here just to sit and admire the bench."

"The bench" was what the Stubbses called their homeplace. The buildings didn't sit upon a bench, but old Sam had been calling their wide swale in the hills that so long everyone else had also adopted the term. Sheriff Holbrook fished out his tobacco sack and went to work making a smoke.

" 'Came to talk to you about Holfinger," he said, lighting up and exhaling. "About that warning someone gave him last fall when they shot his steer."

"All right," Sam said pleasantly, not the least surprised. "Let's talk about it, Tim. You want to start off?"

"No. You start off, Sam."

"All right. In the first place he dumped three thousand head on us out of the blue sky. In the second place his riders got a bad habit of pushing local cattle away from the waterholes. In the third place, Tim, he don't make any effort to be decent, he don't even live out here. He stays in town an' once in a while rides to his cow-camp, gives his Texans their wages, their orders, and rides back to sit around the saloons playin' poker and talkin' big."

"That's hardly much reason to make trouble, Sam," murmured Sheriff Holbrook. "Some men don't like the cow-camp life. They prefer poker and loafin'."

"All right. But what about him over-stockin' our range?"

"It's not your range, Sam, it's free-graze. It's open range from here to the horizon in all directions."

"Then why don't he go somewhere else?"

Holbrook sat a little straighter in his chair. "Sam, *free-graze* means just exactly that. He doesn't *have* to go anywhere else. That's the law. If he stays here he's got as much right as anyone else has to do so."

"Aw hell, Tim," said Sam Stubbs, eyeing the lawman, "you know a damned sight better'n that. *He* didn't develop the water here. *He* didn't clean the rustlers an' renegades out'n these hills. *He* don't care a tinker's damn about conservin' the grass. Tim, you look me in the eye and tell me Arnold Holfinger's got as much right in the Buckskin Hills as I have."

Sheriff Holbrook squirmed. "The law says he has, Sam. It's not up to me to say what's right and what's wrong. The Territorial Legislature makes the law, I only enforce it."

"Tim, you look me in the eye an' tell me Holfinger's got as much right as the Stubbses have."

Holbrook stood up and killed his smoke. "Sam," he exclaimed. "No more shootin' of his critters, and no more warnings like that last one. If you want him out of your hills figure some *legal* way to accomplish it."

"You haven't looked me in the eye, Tim."

"No," exclaimed Sheriff Holbrook, "and I'm not going to either. Just do us both a favour, Sam. No more trouble. I mean it. In the first place you're puttin' me in a hell of a spot. In the second place you're under-estimatin' Arnold Holfinger. Now mind your manners, Sam, doggone it, and I'll see you again one of these days—social-like."

CHAPTER TWO

CHARLEY PARTRIDGE who ran the general store in Bull-head was a quick, high-strung, shrewd man of fifty who knew everyone for a hundred miles around, and also either knew their business or could guess it because he was also the local banker.

There was no bank at Bullhead, just Charley's mighty Detroit safe; a huge steel box painted battle-ship grey, water-chilled in the making to resist dyna-mite, drills, bullets, the wiles of the craftiest outlaw, and to make doubly certain it was impregnable Charley had the thing bolted to a three-foot-thick slab of mortar in the back of his store. In that safe were the funds, the books, even the family papers, of most of the cowmen for a goodly distance roundabout. It lent Charley a rare distinction in the countryside too; he was the combination of purveyor and guardian to the cattlemen. He also happened to be an inveterate gossip, so when Tim Holbrook returned from the Stubbs ranch, Charley was waiting for Tim over at the ugly, squat, massive-walled jailhouse with an interest-ing bit of gossip.

"There's a feller campin' in the southward hills," he reported. "He never stays in one camp more'n two days, Tim, and he stays to the ridges. The Spangler boys have cut his sign on their part of the range and once they got a glimpse of him. He wears a bone-handled sixgun and everywhere he goes, even down to the water with his horse, he carries his carbine."

Holbrook was interested. "Did they get a look at his face, Charley?"

"No, they said not. He keeps watch like an eagle, Tim. They figure he's a wanted man or he wouldn't be actin' like he does."

"That's why I asked if they'd seen his face. I got a pile of wanted posters that might have him among 'em."

Charley had said all he had to say. He went to the office door, opened the panel and as a parting word, said, "Tim, you better have a look. Remember, I got a heap of money and valuables in my safe."

"One man couldn't bust that box, Charley."

"I know. But he could sure set fire to my store tryin'. Anyway, if he's an outlaw he means no good hangin' around. You goin' to have a look?"

Holbrook nodded. There were times, him being a calm, quiet man, that Charley Partridge's type irritated him. "I'll ride out and have a look around. But if I were you I wouldn't worry about your safe."

That same day, though, the Spanglers rode into Bull-head. They were heavy-set, large men, stolid, straight-forward, taciturn. The kind of men who, in their late thirties, had got into a way of life that required of them very little imagination, very little originality. They turned their cattle out in the early spring, salted and tended them throughout the growing season, then sold the calf crop in the fall, put their money in Charley Partridge's steel box, and hibernated for the balance of the year.

Ariel was the elder; he was beginning to grey a little. Clay was the younger. But there wasn't more than two years between them. They acted alike and thought alike. Folks said when Ariel coughed Clay spat.

It was Ariel who walked into the jailhouse and nodded first. Clay came in second and also nodded. Sheriff Holbrook mumbled a greeting and flagged the brothers to chairs which they didn't take. Ariel said, " 'Reckon Charley told you about the stranger on our range, Tim."

"He did," replied the lawman. "As a matter of fact he told me just a little while ago. Why? Have you seen him again?"

"No," said Clay heavily. "We saw another one."

Now Holbrook's gaze sharpened slightly. "Another what?" he demanded.

"Another stranger ridin' the ridges and keepin' to himself. This one's got a bedroll behind his saddle and full bags on each side of his saddle. We saw him sittin' on a slope with a spyglass, watchin' the Stubbs place. Big man, Tim; not heavy but tall. He wears black; black shirt, black hat, dark pants, an' his horse is black. Good animal, too, powerful."

"When did you see this one?" Tim inquired.

"This mornin'. We were checkin' the boundary makin' sure our cattle didn't drift too far over onto the Stubbs' range. There he was, spyin' on the buildings from up the slope a mile away."

Holbrook knew these two taciturn men. "So you back-tracked him a-ways," he said, making a statement of it.

Ariel nodded. "Naturally. He had a new camp about six miles off down in a canyon where the trees are thick an' there's a spring."

"Anything interesting in the camp?"

"We didn't go down. Tim, if there's two of them fellers there just might be more too. Furthermore, if they're cattle rustlers we figured you'd better make the investigation. It's the right time of year; rustlers can pick up a bunch when folks've turned out, knowin' they won't be missed for a spell, and drive them clean over the Rockies. There's feed everywhere in the spring-time."

"I'll have a look," said Tim. "Meanwhile, you boys keep a sharp watch. If you spot any more of them, or if you see anything else, come in and let me know."

The Spanglers left. Tim Holbrook heaved a mighty sigh and took his carbine from its wall-peg, seated himself at his desk and got out all his cleaning paraphernalia. The worst trouble he'd had in Bullhead in three years had been when two of Holfinger's Texans got drunk and went on a rampage through town. That had been the autumn before and it hadn't amounted to much. Holfinger had posted bond and so far the circuit judge hadn't arrived in Bullhead so that's how things still stood. He still had Holfinger's money, the Texans were still loose, and nearly everyone had forgotten about the entire episode.

Sometimes a man could feel trouble coming. If he had Tim Holbrook's bump of perspicacity, he could just about circle a number on the calendar and say trouble would arrive on that day. Some men had that gift and some didn't. Also, sometimes a lawman could tell from the way the weather fell whether he'd have a good year or a bad one. It wasn't, as some folks thought, the bad, drought years, that saw an increase in trouble. It was invariably the good, green years when there was plenty of money floating around; when everyone seemed more relaxed and easy, that something like enterprising horse thieves or cattle rustlers showed up to get their share of the affluence.

Tim didn't exactly know why that was, he only knew that it was a predictable fact of life. As for the pair of shy gents the Spangler brothers had seen, if they were rustlers there'd have to be more than just the pair of them. Two men, no matter how good they were at their work, couldn't run off a very big herd of cattle.

No, it had to be something else. And finally, what the Spanglers hadn't recognised struck Tim Holbrook as relevant. They'd reported to him that the one with the brass spyglass had a new camp back in the hills. They'd told Charley Partridge the other one—the one with the bone-handled sixgun—had made several camps, which meant in simple terms, the bone-handled one had been in the Buckskin Hills for maybe several weeks, while the spyglass-one, had only just arrived. Of course it wasn't impossible that they hadn't come here by some pre-arrangement. But Sheriff Tim didn't think so. Outlaws making a rendezvous in new country don't camp apart. It's against their gregarious nature.

So, what Tim had, was two strangers acting like outlaws, hiding out in the same general area, who were strangers to each other, and that complicated things for one lawman who couldn't be in two places at the same time.

He finished with the carbine and sat through the evening going over his stack of wanted flyers memorising faces. Tim Holbrook was a methodical man. He also, although people who saw him for the first time never really believed it, was deadly fast and mortal accurate with a sixgun. Sometimes Nature played that joke; put the heart of a lion and the perfect co-ordination of a killer under a nondescript hide. It was one of the fateful ironies of frontier life that you couldn't sometimes tell just by looking at a man, how dangerous or deadly he might be.

John Bronson was a good example of that. John had a small ranch in the hills which he'd inherited from his dead parents. He was a dark, swarthy man of solid build and genial disposition who, some hinted, had Injun blood, and therefore was capable of savage fury. But John was a hard-worker and seldom even visited the saloons in Bullhead before he married the waitress from Grace Morgan's café in town. But afterwards he hardly came to town at all. Still, he was big and dark and hard as iron from rough labour. If ever a man had the appearance of being gun-handy and dangerous to cross, it was John Bronson. But Tim Holbrook, a life-long student of men—in his line of work he had to be to stay alive—knew how easily John laughed and how he winced from violence of any kind.

Jim Sargent and Joe Cane were different. They ranched farther back in the Buckskin Hills. Neither was married and both were rangy, rawboned men with the tell-tale yeasty glance that clearly warned of a fierce temper. They too worked hard, but also, they drank hard. When folks said there was such a thing as an attraction of opposites they didn't have Jim and Joe in mind, for they were alike even to build, and they were fast friends. They worked together as a team at roundup time, they came to Bullhead to get their supplies in the same wagon, and when they tied one on at the *Blue Mule Saloon*, they did it standing side by side at the bar.

Tim Holbrook had only once in the past six years had to intervene when Jim and Joe came to town. Usually, they minded their own business and if left alone, let others alone. That one intervention had been occasioned when Holfinger's Texans had first arrived in the Bullhead country powder-dry and with a deep-down itch for action after being on the trail for two months steady without a release, they had made the mistake of jostling Jim and Joe during one of their solemn occasions of drinking in the *Blue Mule*.

The Texans were noisy, high-spirited men. Jim and Joe drank as though it were a solemn duty; they stood at the bar without a word passing between them, taking turns setting up the drinks. When they got jostled they eyed the strangers but said nothing until the jostling began to get a little out of hand, then they'd turned, still without a comment passing between them, and had knocked down two of Holfinger's riders, stepped over their bodies and had gone after the others like a pair of wildmen.

Joe Annakin, the *Blue Mule's* proprietor-bartender, had decked Joe with his wagon spoke, kept under the bar for just such emergencies, and Tim Holbrook, drawn to the scene by the tumult, had put Jim Cane down from behind with his pistol barrel.

After that Holfinger's Texans were careful who they jostled, and Jim and Joe didn't return to Bullhead for a drinking bout until nearly everyone had forgotten that little affair.

Tim had a saying: people came in endless variety although they looked pretty much the same, and that's what made them interesting. It also was what kept a lawman in a frontier border town on his toes. Or, as Grace Morgan, Tim's long-time girl friend, said, "If Tim doesn't take off that badge, one of these days we'll have the biggest funeral in Bullhead the town's ever seen."

Grace was a buxom woman in her thirties. She'd arrived in Bullhead two years before from no one knew where—not even nosy Charley Partridge—and had opened her café. She was a handsome woman, with a thick mane of sorrel hair and teeth as white as snow. Her eyes were green; she used them to chill many a rangerider to the marrow. At first she'd even regarded Tim Holbrook icily, but that had changed the night he took her to the volunteer fire brigade's annual dance and box social. Tim had been a perfect gentleman. After that they went buggy riding on summer nights, when he had the time, and in the winter they visited over her café counter.

But since John Bronson had married the little waitress she'd imported from Tucson, Grace hadn't been able to leave the café. Tim coaxed her to import another one but Grace said only a fool made the same mistake twice, and returned to running the café by herself. In the largely womanless Bullhead country, pretty little waitresses didn't stay long.

Tim put up his cleaned and oiled carbine and sauntered through soft shadows to Grace's place for his supper. It was his one predictable ritual and he loved it.

CHAPTER THREE

THE STOCK DETECTIVE named Brent visited Bullhead one night and left a slip of paper shoved under the door of Arnold Holfinger's room at the town boarding-house—politely called the "hotel". He could have found Holfinger at the *Blue Mule* but he evidently didn't care to make the effort. He rode in late, left his note and rode out again. If anyone noticed him no one afterwards mentioned it.

But when Holfinger read that note, he waited until the following dawn, then rode out of town towards the Buckskin Hills. When he returned later in the day, via his cow-camp and a visit there with his rangeboss, he was subdued and thoughtful. Something was going on. Not among the ranchers; or at least he didn't believe it was anything they had organised, but still, Brent had seen a second watcher in the hills, a furtive horseman, he'd told Holfinger, who seemed to know every nook and cranny, for when Brent tried to stalk him, the stranger just rode over a hill and dropped from sight, which made Brent want to know if Holfinger had sent someone to spy on him, or if Holfinger had any knowledge that the cattlemen had also hired an assassin of their own.

The sheriff was nigging out at the liverybarn when Holfinger rode in. They exchanged a nod and a pleasant word, then Holfinger strolled over and asked if Tim was going into the westerly hills. Tim said that he was, but that's all he said. He wasn't convinced that the strangers he'd heard about might not have something to do with Holfinger or his Texans.

"I just came back from there," mused the dandified Texan. "And funny thing, Sheriff, I cut a lot of fresh sign of someone making different camps up there."

Tim dropped his stirrup and snapped the latigo. "That so," he said, turning slowly to regard the cowman. "Probably some of the local boys out salting, or maybe calving out their heifers."

"No," persisted Holfinger. "I doubt that. Seemed more like it was someone travelling through. Or maybe hiding out. Possibly even sizing up the herds. A rustler maybe."

"Just one?" asked Tim thoughtfully.

"Yeah. Just this one set of tracks and the little camps where one man had slept and hobbled his horse."

"Well," said Tim, turning back. "I'll have a look around while I'm out there. Where did you pick up the sign?"

"Southward and westward."

"That'd be over on Sam Stubbs' range," said Holbrook, as he swung up across leather. "You out visitin' with old Sam?"

Holfinger's face briefly clouded. He had no use for Sam Stubbs and Holbrook knew it. "Hardly," he grunted, and walked on out of the barn.

Holbrook turned his horse, rode out into the roadway and pensively watched Holfinger disappear through the batwing doors of the *Blue Mule*. If the Texan hadn't gone to see Sam, what had taken him out of his own preserve to the Stubbs' place? And one more thing; how come Holfinger to see only one set of marks left in the hills when, if he'd gone southward towards the Spangler range, he'd have just about had to have seen those other tracks as well?

That was interesting.

Tim swung to the left half-way through town making for the broad prairie westward which fetched up against the Buckskin Hills some miles off. It was a pleasant spring-time morning. There were meadow-larks in the grass and a winy scent to the air. Visibility was perfect for ten miles in all directions. Northward, the eternal gloominess of mountain slopes spiked with giant pines and firs seemed much closer than they actually were. Southward where the land distantly and gradually changed until only the sands of an arid desert remained, there was a far-away smokiness caused by rising heat.

In the intervening distance between town and the Buckskin Hills, cattle grazed far out, half wild and constantly alert. They wore two block letters on their left ribs—A H for Arnold Holfinger. They didn't run from Holbrook but neither did they permit him to get closer than gunshot. Where he left the plain and pushed up into the hills there was an old trail, widened by hand labour in places so that a wagon could just barely squeeze through. Once, that had been known as the Sam Stubbs road. Then just the Stubbs road. Finally it was called just the road. The moment he got up in there sunshine winked out and a permeating morning coolness prevailed. He knew the hills, so when a south-ward trail forked off he took it. This was the way to the Spangler place.

But he didn't go to the ranch, he instead headed for a low rise, left his horse just below its top-out, and crawled up the last twenty yards to lie flat with only his head showing so that he could see around without perhaps being seen himself.

There was a little cold fire on the next hill. It showed as a dark blotch in the surrounding greenery. He went back, mounted, and rode boldly on up to that place. It was an old camp. Maybe two, three weeks old. One man had spent the night here. He sat for a while considering the countryside. The Spangler place was southwestward. If whoever had made that camp had been spying on the Spangler brothers he wouldn't have stopped here, he'd have ridden to one of the closer top-outs.

The trail was lost but on a hunch Holbrook turned southward and rode through cloud-shadows until he found two more of those cold camps. At the last one he picked up an empty tobacco sack. With that in his pocket he turned westward. The next little solitary camp had been behind the rearward hill overlooking the Spangler ranch. But the camp after that was northward in the direction of the Stubbs' ranch.

Tim nooned beside a spring and had a cigarette for dinner. One thing he was certain of; whoever this phantom was, he wasn't out to kill either the Spangler boys or the Stubbses. Another thing was also certain; he wasn't just a rider passing through. He'd been in the hills for several weeks now. Evidently he wasn't looking for work or he'd have ridden into one of the ranches. That didn't leave many alternatives for Tim to dwell upon.

He abandoned this loner's trail, and rode around the hills overlooking the Stubbs' place until he found the slope where a man had been sitting only a day or two before. There, he discovered something interesting. This second phantom had a wide stride. Where the heel of one boot had dug in and the toe of the accompanying foot had scuffed dirt, Tim had to stretch far out to match that stride. Big stride meant big man.

He went westerly, deep into the hills on this new trail, and because it was much fresher there wasn't much difficulty. He even found the hidden camp the Spanglers had spoken of, down in a draw where black-oaks grew as thick as hair on a dog's back because there was a spring down there.

Here, he substantiated his earlier observation by strolling back and forth to find smooth limbs where this second stranger had hung his effects. Only a tall man hung things that far off the ground.

But of this one there were only footprints and the hidden camp to go by. This one threw nothing down. Tim had a smoke in mid-afternoon on the same westerly trail. A veteran of the backtrails knew how to hide sign and bury tins emptied of their food. This second one, Tim told himself, was the dangerous one. Not the first one who senselessly cast aside an empty tobacco sack. This second one *was* trouble. The first one *maybe* was trouble.

He was passing across an open hillside and caught, from the edge of his eye, a sharp flash of reflected sunlight from over across a cleft a mile and more to his right. He kept his horse walking along and moved only his head. He was being watched through a spyglass. He had enough of his upper body swung away from that watcher so that he knew his badge would not show, but all the same he reached up surreptitiously and removed the badge with his off hand, dropped it into a vest pocket and used the same hand to tilt back his hat as he slouched along. From that far off about all the spyglass would reveal was that he was a lone horseman moving from west to east through the hills. His face wouldn't be clear this far off, so he could be any of the local men looking after his stock. At least he sincerely hoped that spying watcher arrived at that conclusion, and he rode along casually to heighten the impression.

He was confident the watcher was the second phantom. The fact that he was farther west, back near the farthest reaches of the Stubbs' range, made Tim speculate on his purpose for being there. First, he'd spied on the Stubbs' ranch. Now he was still on Stubbs' range, but spying on riders passing across it. The sane conclusion to that was simple: *This* one was interested in the Stubbses.

He let his horse choose its own downward trail after crossing the dome of the hill where he'd been watched. When the beast was down near the bottom again, Sheriff Holbrook didn't dismount to slip back and observe his observer. He didn't even turn northwestward and try for a closer look. He simply let the horse amble along on its homeward trail.

He left the hills by the same trail he'd used to enter them. He saw several horsemen driving those AH cattle up-country but they were too far off to identify. They'd be Holfinger's Texans, though, Holbrook was certain of that. What he'd have liked to have known, however, was exactly how many of them were with the cattle. It had not escaped him that the smouldering feud between Sam Stubbs and Arnold Holfinger just very well could be behind those phantom horsemen in the hills, and if this were so, considering how those two strangers were acting, it was highly likely they were hired assassins.

Holfinger, Tim was satisfied, was not above hiring a

secret killer. Sam Stubbs too might do that, but it wasn't quite in keeping with Sam's character as Tim Holbrook knew it. Still, Tim had lived just long enough not to categorise people so that he constricted them within behaviour patterns. *Anyway*, under adequate stress and placed in the right circumstance, any man alive would hire a killer, and the Lord knew, there were plenty of gunmen around waiting to be hired.

He saw Bullhead soften under the massive blow of a violent sunset; turn coppery-red in the pleasant gloaming. It was a drowsy little place; he liked it that way and wished it would remain that way. But it would not. No town, even those civilised eastern towns, were never wholly peaceful and quiet, but expecting a place like Bullhead, Arizona Territory, down near the explosive Mexican border, in the heart of the southward cow country, to be permanently serene was about like expecting Charley Partridge to stop worrying even when there wasn't anything in particular for him to worry about.

Tim left his horse for the liverybarn hostler to care for and went across to the *Blue Mule* for a cool beer. Holfinger was at the bar having something a little stronger when Holbrook came in. He waited, then said, as Tim signalled for his beer, that the sheriff must have made quite a ride of it, up there in the Buckskin Hills.

Tim put down his coin and lifted the beer. He drank half of it before putting the glass down or replying. "It's not really that hot out," he told Holfinger. "I'm just naturally thirsty."

Holfinger kept studying Holbrook. "Have a good ride?" he asked. "See anything worth noticing?"

Tim belched *sotto*. "I saw those little camps you mentioned before I rode out. That's about all."

"Curious about that," murmured the tall Texan, turning his whisky glass in a little pool of dampness. "What do you make of it, Sheriff?"

"Nothing. Maybe a rider lookin' the land over for work or sizing up the prospects for homesteading. Maybe some local feller too far from home at the end of the day to ride back, so he bedded down where night caught him. Nothing important."

Holfinger continued twisting and turning his glass, his eyes squeezed nearly closed, his lipless mouth sucked back into a flat, uncompromising line. Through those narrowed lids his eyes craftily glistened. He finally straightened up, tossed off his drink and pushed the glass away as he half-turned and said, "Or, Sheriff, maybe whoever gave me that warning last year is skulkin' around to get a shot at me as I ride to my cow-camp. You ever think of that?"

"No," said Tim candidly. "And if I had I wouldn't be much inclined to take it seriously. Neither should you."

"No? Now tell Cane or Sargent aren't capable of shooting someone they fancy is trespassin' on their land."

Tim looked up, his gaze mild. "Why just them?" he asked. "If you want to scare yourself, Arnold, figure in young Bolton too. And old Sam Stubbs. Maybe even one of your own men who wants to strike out on his own. Or anyone around the country you've won money from in a poker game. Hell, figure in Ariel and Clay Spangler; figure in old Sam's sons or even Joe here, the bartender. A man never knows *all* his enemies, Arnold. He may know the principal ones, but he never knows 'em all." Tim nodded, turned and walked out of the saloon. Something in the back of his mind had firmed up into a solid suspicion. Holfinger had only been interested in one phantom, and yet unless he'd been blind when he'd been up in the hills, he'd have seen the sign of that other one. Why wouldn't a man mention but one particular probable assassin? Because he wasn't the least bit concerned about the other one. And why would that be? *Because he knew who the second one was!*

Charley Partridge was waiting down the roadway for Holbrook. He scarcely let the lawman get down to him before he furtively beckoned Tim inside his store. There were no customers in there, for a change, but then it was getting along towards supper time.

"Sheriff," he said, making somewhat of a pronouncement of it. "A young feller came into town this afternoon while you were gone, bought some tinned goods from me, a box of carbine shells, and five sacks of Bull Durham tobacco. He was a plump stranger so I slipped out an' watched him ride off. He went southward through town, then swung westerly towards the hills."

"Is that a fact?" murmured Tim, and reached up to finger the empty Bull Durham sack in his vest pocket. "What did he look like, Charley? No wait; come on over and go through my poster file an' let's see if you can pick him out."

Partridge nodded his head. "Just as soon as I lock up I'll be right over. Won't take me more'n ten minutes. You wait for me over there, hear?"

"Sure," agreed Holbrook, and walked out of the store.

CHAPTER FOUR

EVENING FELL swiftly in the springtime, although each day it fell a little later. By the time Charley Partridge got over to Holbrook's jailhouse it was dusk. By the time he'd thumbed through the stack of flyers, it was dark out, with Bullhead's usual nightlife beginning to noisily take over.

Sheriff Holbrook said: "Are you plumb sure, Charley?"

Partridge's reply was emphatic. "Sure as I can be, Tim. He's not anywhere among these fellers. At least not among the ones that've got photos on 'em. Now, about the physical descriptions, like I said before, there are a couple in here that could fit him—but in each case the age was wrong. *My* outlaw wasn't more twenty, twenty-two years old."

Holbrook gave it up. "Well, thanks anyway, Charley. Maybe when the next batch of flyers come in he'll be among them."

"Sure," Partridge said, and got up to leave. "Tim, instead of tryin' to make out who he is, seems to me you'd do better to jus' ride out'n surround him—or something."

Holbrook eyed the storekeeper. "Mostly or something," he murmured. "Charley, did I ever tell you how to run your store?"

Partridge went to the door ducking his head up and down. "Awright, awright; forget I even spoke. I'm only thinkin' about them valuables in my safe is all. You got to appreciate the position of responsibility I'm in."

"Oh, I do appreciate that, Charley," said Tim Holbrook warmly. "I do appreciate that." After Partridge left Tim put away his stack of fivers, then he went to his desk and hunted up a cigar he remembered putting in there the previous winter. He found it, dry as dust but still smokable, sat down, propped his booted feet upon an edge of the desk and teetered far back.

Every stranger who entered Charley's store was immediately suspected by Partridge of having dark designs upon Charley's big Detroit safe. It was amusing in a way, and in another way it was confounded annoying, being bothered by Charley every time some drifting cowboy passed through. Still and all, a man had to give old Charley his due; he was the bird-dog of Bullhead: no one came or went—even natives—that he didn't see them, speculate on their purpose for being in town, or out of town, and store up that information like a chipmunk stores acorns in its cheeks.

As for Charley's young stranger who was addicted to Bull Durham tobacco, he was, Tim was satisfied, one of the phantoms. It seemed strongly possible that he'd be the less experienced of the two because of his age. The world was full of hotheads aged twenty-two who went around haranguing for poor causes; sometimes they should be taken seriously, particularly if they happened to be wearing a bone-handled sixgun, because good judgment at age twenty-two was practically nil, while on the other hand perfect eyesight and a steady gunhand were invariably the possession of such young men.

Tim decided he'd take this young man seriously for another reason. He was a genuine enigma. He was no professional killer, or at least if he was he hadn't come to the Buckskin Hills to shoot anyone. It didn't take

two, three weeks to get a chance to back-shoot someone, if that's what a man wanted to do.

The mystery, then, was just why was he here? Why
was he so stealthy in a sort of inexperienced way;
where was he from and who . . .?"

"Daydreaming, Tim?"

He brought his gaze down. Grace was standing in
the doorway with a light shawl across her shoulders.
The way his jailhouse lamplight fell across her upper
body and throat turned the handsome flesh butter-
yellow and made her green eyes like soft emeralds. He
sighed.

"You're a beautiful woman, Grace."

She stepped into the office. "Then why don't you
ask me to marry you?" she said.

He brought his feet down, swung the chair so he
could see the full length of her, and said, "Well, before
I take a step like that I got to know—is the café
making money?" His expression was as solemn as an
owl.

She looked startled at first, then she laughed, moved
in farther and closed the door. "This might be your
last chance, Tim. I might search for a younger man."

He gravely inclined his head, got up to fetch her a
chair and said as he brought one forward, "There are
drawbacks, Grace. Young bucks are demanding. Now
us older fellers—we know how to appreciate a handsome female like you."

As she sat she said, "Tim, I saw Charley Partridge
leave here a while back. Was he telling you fresh
gossip or did he mention a youngster who rode into
town this afternoon?"

"The latter," murmured Tim, sitting back down at
his desk. "Why?"

"Well. I saw him too, and if Charley Partridge was trying to make trouble for that young cowboy he ought to be horsewhipped."

Tim's brows lifted. "Why, Grace? I mean, what's there to get upset about? You know Charley. So do I. So does everyone else around the country. No one gets too upset about his kind of talk. As for the young stranger—it happens I'm interested in strangers right now."

Grace's red hair shone a burnished coppery hue when she lowered her head while examining the fringe of her shawl. "What's one stranger more or less?" she murmured.

Tim watched her face. He knew Grace Morgan well enough, and generally, he knew *people* well enough; when someone averted his—or her—gaze while seriously talking to him, he wondered a little.

"Strangers can be a peck of trouble, Grace, or they can be drifters passing through. I make it a point of trying to decide which."

"But this young man, what trouble could he make?"

"He could kill someone, for one thing, or he could have some crazy notion about Charley's safe. Or he could even be looking over the cattle with some idea of runnin' off a few head."

She raised her eyes to his face. "No, Tim; he's not that kind."

"No? How do you know that, Grace?"

She got up, turned towards the door and said, "I told you. I saw him too. He's clean looking and wholesome. You know the kind, Tim. A young cowboy . . ." She put forth a hand to the latch. "I closed the café early tonight. There wasn't much business anyway." She

B

faced him. "Why don't you ask me to go buggy-riding with you this evening?"

He jack-knifed up out of the chair. "Sure," he murmured. "I'll go get a rig and meet you at your place in half an hour." He held the door for her and afterwards gently closed it.

Where, he wondered, did the powerfully protective female urge to protect the young end, and the equally as powerful urge to admire someone of the opposite sex begin? Grace was leery of men; she'd demonstrated that many times since arriving in the Bullhead country. She was a mature, full woman. If she'd been a young girl he could have understood this sudden switch. But she *wasn't* a young girl, and furthermore young cowboys came and went like falling leaves. Why should this particular one hold such a solid interest for her?"

He went to the lamp, blew down the mantle to plunge his jailhouse office into darkness, then returned to the door and left the building. He hadn't taken fifty steps when two nearly identical shadows moved out of the night to intercept him. One of them called from the roadway.

"Sheriff . . ."

Tim turned. It was difficult to make out their faces in the gloom but he knew their builds. Joe Cane and Jim Sargent. When they stepped up onto the sidewalk he caught the scent of liquor.

"Come to town earlier to look you up," Cane said, his pugnacious features hatbrim-shadowed.

"I've been here most of the evening," Tim said. "What's on your minds?"

"Sheriff," stated Joe Cane, "there's somethin' funny goin' on out on the range." Cane turned. "You tell him," he said to the rawboned man standing there beside him.

Sargent nodded. "This mornin' I was headin' through the hills for Joe's place, Sheriff. We figured to do a little sashayin' around to see where the cattle was driftin' to. All of a sudden I come around the slope of a hill into a shady canyon, you see, and here's this big black horse drowsin' in the shade of an oak tree."

"Saddled?" Tim asked.

"Yes, he was saddled, bridled, and there was a bedroll behind the cantle an' a rifle in the boot. It sort of stopped me, you see, because I know most of the horses folks ride in the hills, and this here one had a brand I never seen before. While I was sittin' there lookin', I got to wonderin' if maybe the horse didn't belong to one of those Texans Holfinger's got ridin' for him. I was thinkin' so hard I never even heard a sound until this big feller in a black hat steps up behind me and says, 'Lose somethin', mister?' I looked around. He had a spyglass under one arm and a .45 in his fist."

"You ever see him before, Jim?"

"Nope. Never in my life, Sheriff. An' like I said, he just come out of nowhere."

"What'd he look like?"

"Tall, like I just said, and wearin' a black shirt an' black hat. Looked to be maybe thirty-forty years old, and he's a stock detective."

Tim Holbrook's eyes widened. "A what? Did he tell you that?"

"He sure did, after he put up his gun and went over to untie his horse. Told me he'd been hired to watch for rustlers in the hills. I asked him who hired him an' he just looked at me real dead-pan, and never answered. He got atop his horse and said, 'Cowboy, just make sure you don't get *your* rope on the wrong calf an' you'll have nothin' to worry about'. Then he rode up the slope and never once looked back. I sat there a while thinkin' that over, but by the time I'd recovered from my surprise and got good an' mad at what he'd hinted, why he was gone over the hilltop."

Tim gazed at Sargent and at Joe Cane. He now had a good description of the second phantom as well as the first one, and was more than ever satisfied that it was this second one he had cause to worry about. *This* one undoubtedly was the killer.

Cane said, "Sheriff, stock detectives leave a bad smell in my nose. Wasn't too long ago the stories that come out of Wyoming had them fellers doin' a sight more on the range than just huntin' cow thieves."

Tim knew about the Powder River War too. Every newspaper in the country had carried grisly stories of that bloody fight. But he also knew something else; stock detectives didn't ride a range unless someone hired them to, and from what he'd earlier surmised while drinking a beer at the *Blue Mule*, he thought he had an idea who that 'someone' might be.

"I'll look into it," he told Sargent and Cane. "And you two might keep an eye peeled in case this stock detective stays in the country. By the way—was he north of the Stubbs' place, Jim?"

Sargent nodded. "Yeah. I'd say he just come down off a sidehill over there."

"About what time was it you ran into him?"

Sargent shrugged. Like most rangemen the hour of the day was not important. Each day had two parts: morning and afternoon. Other than that they would often guess the correct time an hour short or an hour long. "A little past mid-afternoon I reckon, Sheriff."

Tim had seen this same man at about the same time, and he'd been upon that northward slope watching Holbrook through his spyglass, so evidently after the stock detective had seen Tim, he'd ridden down into a southward draw to do some more spying, and that was when and where he'd been run into by Jim Sargent.

Tim glanced over at the café A faint glow showed from a rear room where Grace's quarters were. He sighed. "You fellers step into the jailhouse with me," he said. "I'd like Jim to look through some wanted flyers and see if he recognises that stock detective."

Cane and Sargent were willing. Tim made some rapid calculations and came up with an unpleasant answer: Grace was going to be pacing the floor getting madder by the minute because it had taken Charley Partridge a full hour to look through that same stack of flyers. He turned with resignation and led the way back to his office. As he lit the lamp Jim Sargent removed his hat and Joe Cane drew up a cane-bottomed chair. They didn't either of them seem in the slightest hurry.

It was a fruitless search and an hour later Jim leaned back and shook his head. "He ain't here, Sheriff, I can tell you that for a fact, an' I'm not likely to forget that face either. He was a feller as big or maybe even bigger'n Joe an' me. He had a clipped way of talkin', like he said just exactly what he had to an' no more. He had a sharp, steady way of lookin' at you, like maybe he was sizin' you for a coffin or something." Sargent stood up, yawned, stretched, and stepped away from the desk. "You come out our way tomorrow, Sheriff, an' I'll show you the exact spot where I run onto him. Maybe we can pick up his trail from there."

Tim was non-committal about riding back into the hills the following day and eased the two cattlemen out of his office. For the second time as he blew out the lamp and left his office, he was thinking some uncharitable thoughts about someone.

If it was Arnold Holfinger who'd imported that killer into the Buckskin Hills, he had to know, and fast. Men like this black-hatted stranger didn't work cheap and when they hit a place, or a man, they hit hard. They disliked hanging around a country very long, for excellent reasons.

He walked out of the office and started up towards the liverybarn for the second time. He was half-way there when he saw Grace bearing down on him from the north with her shawl held close and her head thrust forward. Funny thing about a mad woman; they put a man in mind of fighting roosters.

CHAPTER FIVE

SAM STUBBS sent his youngest son, Seldon, to ask Tim to come to the Stubbs' place the next day. All Tim could get from Seldon was that the old man was grimfaced and grumpy about something.

"Whenever something's botherin' paw," explained Seldon, "he just turns real quiet. You can't hardly get a word out of him. He looks like a thundercloud in the face and doesn't say scarcely a word."

Tim knew; he'd seen old Sam mad a few times over the years. As they loped out of Bullhead Tim cast around in his mind for the reasons which might be behind this summons. One thing he was thoroughly satisfied about; Sam Stubbs didn't send for the law unless he had damned good reason for doing so.

"Had any trouble on the range?" he asked.

Seldon's reply was almost casual, "Well, no more'n usual, Sheriff. Holfinger's critters are grazin' deeper across our grass. We've been pushin' them back the last few days." Seldon gave his wide shoulders a little shrug about that. "Seems that's gettin' to be part of our everyday work. No; I doubt if that's what's botherin' paw."

Seldon was partly right. When they reached the ranch Sam was on the front porch rocking in his personal chair and puffing his pipe. He sent his son back to work with a wave of one hand and invited Tim up to sit with him. After Seldon had departed old Sam removed his pipe, scored a bull's-eye on a big red geranium with an amber stream, and set the pipe upon a railing with the sweeping movement of a ship's captain clearing his decks for action.

"Tim," he abruptly said, his voice sharp and incisive. "I made up m'mind after you was here last to do like you said—keep peace with them damned Texans." He reached down where a soiled rag lay, picked it up and tossed it into Holbrook's lap. "But, Tim, there's got to be a limit to a man's patience and this here is my limit. Go ahead, unwrap that thing an' look at it."

Holbrook unfolded the rag. A pair of shaggy red ears neatly cut from the head of a beef critter lay there. Tim wasn't familiar with the earmarks in the Bullhead country although he knew every brand. These particular ears had an undercut fishhook. He raised his eyes. "Yours?" he asked.

"Damned right that's our mark. My other son found that critter late last night right after he heard a gunshot when he was ridin' for home after dark from searchin' for strays. He went back, found the critter, cut off the ears an' fetched 'em to me."

"Last night, Sam? Seldon didn't know about it."

Sam spat again over the railing into the geranium bed. "Seldon's young and hot-tempered," he said. "I didn't want him to know. Now Tim, that critter was shot on our range, so there wasn't any reason for it. A A man's got reason to figure his cattle are safe on his own land."

"Anyone see who shot the animal, Sam?"

"No. Like I just told you, it was dark." Sam fished in a pocket and held out his palm. "But this was lyin' not a hundred feet away."

It was an empty .45 calibre pistol casing. Tim smelled it; there was no question about it, the cartridge had very recently been fired. He held it up to examine the way the firing pin struck the cap. Sometimes—not often, but sometimes—it was possible to match a gun to a fired shell.

"That was Holfinger's doings, Tim, sure as I'm alive an' kickin'," exclaimed the old cowman.

Tim lowered the shell and dropped it into a vest pocket. He said, "Now wait a minute, Sam. You said no one saw who shot your critter. Unless you've got something better than just your dislike of Holfinger, you better step easy about accusin' anyone."

Old Sam's fierce, faded eyes gleamed craftily. "You want proof," he said, "I'll give it to you. Before I sent Seldon to town for you, I sent my other boy to backtrack that assassin this morning before the dew was off the grass. He trailed that feller right back to Holfinger's cow-camp. What d'you think of that?"

Tim stood up and tossed the rag with that pair of severed ears to the porch floor. "I'll go look around," he said. "But I want your word you'll keep your boys away from those Texans."

"Tim, by golly, my boys got as much right as . . ."

"Sam, damn it all, you listen to me. Last year someone pot-shot one of the Holfinger's critters. I'm not saying the Stubbses did it. I don't know who shot that steer and right now I don't care who did it. But if Holfinger's men are getting their revenge you'd better think carefully about what could come of all this, and ask yourself one question: which is more important, a couple of dead steers—or some dead men, maybe one or both of your sons included." Sheriff Holbrook stepped off the porch and went out to his horse. As he untied the reins and flung them up he looked back. Old Sam was reaching for his pipe on the porch railing. "And, Sam," he said, "don't go stirrin' up the other ranchers over this. It's just not worth a fight."

Sam struck a match and puffed hard a moment, his eyes squinted against pungent smoke. "It's not the steer, Tim, it's the principle of the thing. A man's cattle should be safe on his own range." Sam shook the match and settled back in his chair. "I've already sent my oldest boy to see Jim Sargent, Joe Cane, John Bronson and the Spangler boys. If Holfinger's damned Texans will shoot one of my critters, what's preventin' them from shootin' other critters?"

"Me," said Tim from the saddle. "I'm on my way to their camp right now." He swung and loped out of the yard with strong morning sunlight across his shoulders and back. Once, a mile out, he spotted a solitary rider loping in the same direction he was taking, but the man was too far ahead to be identified. Still, he speculated grimly that it was probably one of Holfinger's riders. Since there were no AH cattle so close to the Stubbs' home-place, that Texan—if that's who he actually was—probably had been spying on either Sheriff Holbrook or the Stubbs' ranch.

Trouble was coming, he told himself. Two lousy dead steers were going to spark it, neither of them worth more than forty dollars. What a sorry thing to get men shot over.

He kept to the high places angling around sidehills so he could spare his horse the up-and-down climbing. A man accustomed to hill country had more reason to consider his mount's welfare than a rider from the prairies. A tuckered horse couldn't make good time and Tim Holbrook wanted to reach that Texas camp while there were still likely to be men in it.

He made it, but just barely. Holfinger had seven riders working for him under a dark-eyed, thin-lipped, compact Texan named Sartain: Jack Sartain. Tim had reason to know Holfinger's rangeboss. Sartain was an unsmiling, hard-faced man in his early forties with hair as black as night and as straight and coarse as the hair of an Indian. He was mean when he'd been drinking and although Tim had never had any serious trouble with Jack Sartain, he recognised in the dark Texan that peculiar type of man who kept dark secrets locked in his heart.

Sartain was one of those men who gave the impression of being constantly balanced upon the razor's edge of violence. He was an even six feet tall and didn't weigh more than a hundred and sixty pounds fully clothed; he was a rawhide-type man; wiry, perfectly co-ordinated, fast as greased lightning when he wished to be.

It was Sartain who first saw Holbrook approaching across the plateau where the Texans had their cow-camp. He stood beside a saddled horse staring hard for an unmoving moment, then he swung his head and barked something to the other six riders. They all straightened around to also squint out where Holbrook was coming towards them.

The cow-camp was a jumble of horse-gear and bed-rolls, camp equipment beside a canvas-topped old battered wagon, and powdery dust that came to life every time someone took a step. Someone had rigged up a stone-boat with runners under it instead of wheels. Lashed to the stone-boat were two barrels which the Texans used to haul water up atop their hill in. It was a careless camp and had obviously been on the plateau for some length of time. As Tim Holbrook slowed to a walk and passed over the final intervening hundred yards he saw how those seven men were impassively eyeing him. It was one of the facts of a lawman's life that after a while he could sniff the atmosphere like an old hound dog and just about tell what impended. Those Texans for instance, were leery of him. They had something on their minds; something that made them wary of Tim Holbrook's visit to their camp. He thought dourly he knew what it was: a dead steer.

Sartain nodded, just barely, as the sheriff stopped and leaned forward in his saddle. "Out a mite early aren't you?" asked the dark-eyed rangeboss.

"Got reason," said Tim, gazing around all those closed, cautious faces. "Someone shot one of Sam Stubbs' steers last night, Jack."

Sartain had a ready, dry answer. "It happens in this

country, Sheriff. Last fall if you'll recollect, we lost one the same way."

"I remember."

"Care to get down? I think the coffee's still warm."

"No, thanks. Jack, whoever shot that Stubbs' steer did a sorry thing."

"Yeah, I know," purred the dark Texan. "Last year we thought the same way."

Tim let that remark go by. "I've seen a lot of cattle in my time, Jack, and so have you. I've never yet seen any two head worth the life of a man. Have you?"

Sartain didn't answer. He said, "What're you drivin' at, Sheriff?"

"That it's got to stop right here. Otherwise, someone's likely to get hurt. And no two steers on earth are worth a man's life."

"Well," drawled the rangeboss. "That last part's sure true enough. But about it stoppin' right here—are you hintin' maybe some of us had somethin' to do with Stubbs losin' a steer?"

"I'm hinting nothing, Jack. I'm telling you—it's got to stop."

"Suits me, Sheriff. Only you're talkin' to the wrong crew. What you ought to be doin' is goin' around among them hill-billy stockmen farther west. They're the ones that're always aggravatin' things. Not us."

"It takes two, Jack, it always has. One man can't get up much of a battle if no one'll take the opposite side from him."

"That's true," stated Sartain. "But somethin' you got to remember, Sheriff: don't no man take kindly to be scoffed at, ignored in the street or at the bar, or havin' a bunch of backwoodsmen forever pushin' his cattle off range they claim as theirs when it's really all open range."

Tim sat up there considering those hard, tough rangeriders. If there was a sound answer or a ready solution, it escaped him. Part of what Sartain had just said was true. Part of what old Sam Stubbs had said had also been true. This was how range wars began; over two rough-coated two-bit dead steers, but behind those steers lay the simmering antagonisms of two different kinds of men clashing on the same range.

Nothing he could say further was going to make the least impression upon Sartain or his riders. Only the man who gave them orders and paid their wages—Arnold Holfinger—could keep them in line. He'd have a strong talk with Holfinger as soon as he hit town. Meanwhile, he'd try one last time.

"Jack," he said, "the score's even. Last year it was your critter. This year it's Sam Stubbs' critter. As for the range being crowded, that'll take care of itself when you fellers ship out. Meanwhile, all of you keep clear of each . . ."

"Sheriff," Sartain interrupted. "I don't know where you're gettin' your information, but we're not shippin' out. At least we're not shippin' out the cows an' heifers. Mister Holfinger's keepin' back all the bred critters and sellin' only his steers this year. An' another thing, he's bringin' in another thousand bred cows to take the place o' the steers. He was out here last night an' told me that to my face."

Sartain's dark, hooded eyes gleamed with cold amusement. Tim saw that; Sartain was enjoying this. In a veiled and careful manner he was deliberately trying to make the law look poor in front of his cowboys. And he had just succeeded. This was the first

Tim had heard of Holfinger's plan to not only remain in the Buckskin Hills, but to expand his herd as well. And that, no mistake about it, meant real trouble.

He turned his horse without a nod or a word and rode southward down across the cow-camp plateau. Near the farthest roll where the land dipped, he heard someone back there make a ringing laugh. He didn't look back.

By the time he got back within sight of Bullhead it was early afternoon. Dust was rising from beneath the huge steel tyres of a freight wagon bringing in supplies.

There was the usual brisk activity. Bullhead was the hub of commerce for a number of miles in all directions. He rode into the liverybarn from out the back, left his horse, and walked over to Grace's place for his mid-day meal. She was still a little miffed at him over the delay he'd caused her the night before, but that dissolved gradually. She sat across the counter from him watching him eat, and after a while asked if he'd been out of town on the trail of that young cowboy they'd talked of last night.

"I wish," he told her over the rim of a coffee cup, "that's all I had to worry about. Have you seen Arnold Holfinger around town this afternoon?"

"He was in here at noon but I haven't seen him since."

Tim finished his meal, dropped a large coin atop the counter, took up his hat and walked out. Grace watched him turn north in the direction of the *Blue Mule Saloon*. She was solemn. She knew Tim Holbrook well enough to recognise that expression of grave concern when he wore it. Somewhere ahead in the pulsing spring-time, trouble lurked. Tim wouldn't look like that unless it did.

CHAPTER SIX

ARNOLD WAS at the far end of the bar amusedly watching two rangemen tugging at the same hat which each drunkenly asserted profanely was his, when Sheriff Holbrook walked in. Those two cowboys recognised the lawman at the same time Holfinger also did. One of them called to him, insisting the other man was attempting to steal his hat. From along the bar and among the gaming tables men looked on in high glee.

Tim took the hat, looked inside the brim, asked which man was named Curly Whitten, and when one of the riders said that was his name, Tim handed him the hat.

"Your name's inside it," he said, and pushed the other cowboy over towards the bar. "Go have a drink," he said.

Holfinger made room for Holbrook as the lawman came down to his end of the bar. The saloon was full of men, noise, and smoke. Tim considered. Holfinger had a half shot-glass of whisky in front of him. "Drink it down," he ordered. "Then walk outside with me."

Holfinger gazed at Holbrook with the final vestiges of his former amusement dying. He silently nodded, flung back his head, downed the liquor and turned from the bar to follow Tim out into the soft, balmy night. They had to veer off to avoid a collision at the doors when three rowdy rangemen barged in loudly talking.

Outside, where the noise still reached, Tim turned and paced along until they were in front of a harness

shop which had a bolted-down bench in front of a
glass window. It was dark there, and gloomy, but it
was also quiet. Southward down the row of store-
fronts there wasn't a single light until the hotel doorway showed, flanked by a pair of lighted lamps.

"What's this all about?" the Texan asked, eyeing
Tim speculatively.

"Someone shot one of Sam Stubbs' steers last night,"
Tim said, facing the taller, leaner man. "I have reason
to believe he came from your cow-camp, Arnold."

"Well," said Holfinger easily. "That shouldn't be
hard to determine, Sheriff. I'll ride out in the morning
and ask Jack if any of the men were absent after . . ."

"You'd be wasting your time. I already talked to
Jack. He wouldn't say who shot that steer if he knew."

Holfinger's gaze hardened slightly. He didn't seem
to like the sheriff's attitude. "Now wait a minute," he
said softly, and got no further.

"Arnold, *you* wait a minute. I'm not going to beat
around the bush with you. The time for that is just
about past. I don't give a damn who shot that steer.
But I *do* give a damn about you importing stock detectives who also happen to be bushwhackers."

Holfinger's eyes drew out narrow. He kept studying
Tim Holbrook through the little interval of silence the
lawman permitted to exist after making that statement
about the stock detective. But Holfinger didn't say a
word. He seemed suddenly to be cautious; to be willing
to listen rather than speak.

"You pay that killer off and you get him out of the
country, Arnold. I'm not asking you to do that—I'm
telling you."

Finally, Holfinger said quietly, "Sheriff, I don't know
what you're talkin' about. And furthermore, I don't

think you know either. If you mean that feller who's skulkin' around out on the range, it was me who told you about him. If I'd hired him to come here and shoot someone would I tell you . . .?"

"I'm not talkin' about that feller and you know it, Arnold. I'm talkin' about the feller you *didn't* tell me you'd seen the tracks of on the range. The tall man wearing a black hat and riding a black horse. Your stock detective."

Arnold Holfinger reached inside his coat, drew out a cigar and carefully lit it. He turned, examined the bench, stepped back and sat down upon it crossing one long leg over the other one. He raised his eyes coolly to Sheriff Holbrook's face. "Sheriff," he said, "I don't know what's got you all roiled up, but I sure don't know anything about a stock detective in the hills, and that's a fact."

Tim said, "All right, Arnold. You've had your warning. Now I'll tell you something else. Don't try bringing in any more cattle. If you do someone is going to get killed and it just damned well might be you."

"Whoa," murmured the Texan, removing his cigar. "Whoa up there, lawman. That's free-graze up there. You nor anyone else can keep my cattle or my men out of those damned hills, an' don't you ever try it."

Tim drew in a big breath and slowly let it out. "You're only half right," he said. "I don't have the authority to block the range to your stock or your men. But I can do something just as good, Arnold. I can keep your men out of this town, and I can also keep *you* out. I've got *that* much authority."

Holfinger smoked a moment with his eyes unwaveringly upon Tim Holbrook. Eventually he said, "I see, Sheriff. I see exactly what you're tryin' to do.

You're on the side of those ridgerunners up in the hills; old Stubbs and the rest of that vermin. You've sold out to them and the lot of you have rigged up this scheme for getting my cattle out of the Bullhead country." Holfinger suddenly stood up. He was mad; it showed in the way he thrust his head out when he said, "If I have to I'll hire my supplies freighted in. I'll do one better than that, too. I'll bring in more men. Sheriff, if you want a fight by gawd I'll see that you get a bellyful." Holfinger flung his cigar out into the roadway. "And finally, Holbrook, I don't think you can get the local merchants to go along with that hare-brained scheme anyway. They like my money too much. Now keep out of my way or I'll . . ."

"You'll what," snapped Tim, taking one backward step, his right arm and shoulder settling lower than his left. "What'll you do, Arnold?"

Holfinger was wearing a Prince Albert coat that hung to the hips. Beneath it on the right side was his holstered gun. He had to brush back the coat first, to expose the gun, and that could be interpreted as a signal. He didn't believe he had much to fear from a man as nondescript as Tim Holbrook. Still, he made no move to brush back the coat. He stood a moment gazing at the other man, his arrogant glare slowly turning contemptuous.

"I'll get your badge, Holbrook. That's what I'll do. One way or another I'll get your job if you get in my way. An' you might tell those hill-billy cowmen-friends of yours the next time they push my cattle back off the high hills, I'll settle with them too. Open range means just exactly that, Holbrook. *Open* range. That's the law and I'm damned well within it."

"You're going to cause a war, Arnold."

"Then I'll cause one. We'll let the *federal* law come in here and decide who's right and who's wrong. But don't you try anythin', Sheriff, and that's a warning."

Up the road some men gave quick, startled shouts. Tim could see them over Holfinger's left shoulder. They were moving quickly out into the roadway from in front of the *Blue Mule* where five horsemen were slow-pacing their way down through the shadowy night. At the back of their moving little column the last man was leading a horse with what looked like a pack tied across it.

Those cowboys running forth from the sidewalk in front of the *Blue Mule* suddenly stopped. The horsemen went right past them without a word. Tim Holbrook turned sideways. Arnold Holfinger also turned to watch that silent, shadowy cavalcade come down the road towards them.

Tim recognised big Ariel Spangler in the lead. Just behind Ariel was his brother Clay. Behind Clay riding side by side were Joe Cane and Jim Sargent. The last rider, leading the pack-animal, was Seldon Stubbs. Sheriff Holbrook stepped out into the roadway, turning his back fully upon Arnold Holfinger. The tall Texan remained back where he was, moving only his eyes.

Ariel Spangler saw Tim and halted. Along the southward sidewalk men began to congregate, their voices a low sigh of sound. Ariel leaned from the saddle. "Go take a look," he said to the sheriff. "We were breakin' up a meetin' at the Stubbs' place. Bronson rode out first. There was a gunshot from up the hill behind the Stubbs' buildings. Bronson got it right between the shoulderblades from behind. Go take a look, Sheriff."

Very briefly Tim Holbrook was frozen where he

stood. Ariel Spangler's dry eyes lay upon him with a kind of hard irony. It was almost as though Spangler were accusing *Holbrook* of Bronson's killing. Then he moved; started down toward that led horse. The riders sat their saddles like stone. A few men started forward from the westerly plankwalk and Holbrook snarled at them to get on back where they belonged. This was a quite different Sheriff Holbrook.

He raised the blanket, bent low and peered at the dead man's face. It was young John Bronson all right. He dropped the blanket and looked briefly at the ground. Who would tell John's new little wife?

"Sheriff," said Seldon Stubbs, "it was a right good shot. The moon didn't help much tonight. Neither did the stars. And we couldn't see *him*, up that sidehill, but he could see *us*."

"Yeah," murmured Holbrook. "Seldon, take him over to Doc's place for embalmin', then fetch the others on down to the jailhouse, I'd like to talk to the lot of you."

Seldon nodded. "Sure, Sheriff. Who tells his bride?"

Tim got a little irritable. "You know damned well," he growled. "Now go on."

The riders shuffled on. Over along the sidewalks men drifted away, some back towards the saloons and card rooms, a few on down in the wake of the hill-country cattlemen to learn what else the ranchers knew of this blatant murder.

Holfinger was still over there on the edge of the sidewalk gazing out at Sheriff Holbrook. He'd lit another cigar. Holbrook would have turned away but Holfinger called to him.

"Holbrook. They're half blamin' you for that. How do you like that?"

Tim gazed straight over where Holfinger stood, then he started softly walking in that direction. He didn't say a word, just walked on up where Holfinger teetered upon the edge of the plankwalk, and reached with his left hand, struck with his right. Holfinger dropped his stogie. His hat flew off. He did not seem to actually believe Holbrook would do it until the very last second, and by then he'd waited too long. Holbrook's fist caught him flush in the middle after travelling no further than eighteen inches. It had all the solid heft of the lawman rammed in behind it.

Holfinger's breath broke forth in a loud rush. He jack-knifed forward and Holbrook hooked a vicious little uppercut that dropped the cattleman as though he'd been pole-axed.

Some men farther up the roadway craned around in pure astonishment. Mostly, they were men who had known Tim Holbrook several years and had never in all that time seen him explode. They stood staring.

Holbrook stepped back, surveyed the wreckage, turned his back and went across the road on a diagonal course bound for his jailhouse. There would be repercussions; Holfinger wouldn't accept his being knocked out as final. He was one of those braggart Texans whose pride wouldn't permit him to accept anything as damaging to his public image as a public licking. But right at the moment Tim Holbrook didn't much care. He had his mind made up about Holfinger, but more than that he was satisfied Holfinger was behind whoever had shot John Bronson, and that, Tim Holbrook knew, wasn't final either. Sam Stubbs wouldn't let it end there. He'd been ready to go to war over one shot steer; what his reaction would be to the murder of one of his neighbouring cowmen would be, Tim knew exactly. Time might mellow some old men, but not the rough-tough old Sam Stubbs-type cowmen of this world.

The Spanglers and Joe Cane were waiting outside the office door when Tim reached his jailhouse. They mumbled something about Jim Sargent having gone along with Seldon Stubbs. They did not mention Holbrook's savage attack upon Arnold Holfinger at all.

Tim entered, turned up his lamp, tossed aside his hat and said, "Let's have all of it, boys, right from the start. How come you all to be over at the Stubbs' place?"

Joe Cane said, "Old Sam sent for us. Said it was to be a meetin'. By the time Jim an' I got there—we had the farthest to come—John Bronson and the Spanglers was already there. Old Sam told us about his shot steer. Showed us the ears and said it was time we all commenced patrollin' the range against Holfinger's cattle an' his cow-shootin' Texans. We had a sort of general discussion. Nothin' was really decided on. Jim an' me, we decided the old man was right. But Ariel, Clay and John, well, they wasn't convinced things was likely to get as bad as old Sam said, so we figured to let things slide for a few days before really doin' anythin'."

Tim cocked his head. "Wait a second," he murmured. "Did you boys set up another meetin'?"

Cane nodded. "For next week at the Stubbs' place."

"Well," said Holbrook, "don't have that meeting. If you do someone else is goin' to get it." The men looked at him. "It's an old method those killers use for intimidating folks and keeping them from getting organised."

Clay Spangler said, "You mean—pick us off one at a time?"

Holbrook nodded. At that moment Seldon Stubbs walked in. He was the youngest man in the room, but right then he didn't look very boyish. He simply reached for a chair, swung it and dropped down astraddle of it to look and listen. Holbrook asked Seldon if he'd left John Bronson with the doctor. Seldon solemnly nodded.

"He'll have him cleaned up for delivery to John's widow by morning. Who's going to take him up there, Sheriff?"

Holbrook answered softly. "I will. I'll take Grace with me. His wife's pretty young to take a jolt like this all alone." He turned back to his former topic. "You remember what I said; no more meetings."

Ariel Spangler said, "Sheriff, that tall feller skulkin' around on the range—would he be the bushwhacker?"

Holbrook shrugged. "It's too early to say for certain, Ariel. But I'll tell you one thing. I aim to find out."

"Not alone," stated Cane.

"Yes, alone. That man's got a spyglass. He'd pick up the dust of a posse before it could get within a couple of miles. And you fellers stay out of it. I know how you feel, but stay out of it anyway. You'll get your chance if it proves out he's the killer."

Jim Sargent came in smelling slightly of whisky. He sat down without a word, his rugged features alive with some private thoughts. After the others had talked a little, speculating, swearing, making grisly predictions, Jim said, "Sheriff, them riders of Holfinger's just come in. They're up at the *Blue Mule* commiseratin' with their boss. Sartain's talkin' war against you for knockin' Holfinger down." Jim's fierce gaze danced with a lively interest in Holbrook. "I missed that, but I got to say I'm four-square behind you in it."

"Like I just told the others," stated Holbrook. "You boys keep out of it. If I need help I'll let you know, don't worry, but until I do, mind your own business and *don't* all of you congregate in the same place again. That's how these men work; try for the leaders to break the back of cowman-resistance. Now go on home. *Not* up to the *Blue Mule*, but straight home. Leave Sartain an' Holfinger to me." Holbrook looked at the Spanglers. "You two make certain all of you leave town. Stay away from the *Blue Mule*."

CHAPTER SEVEN

GRACE GOT READY to make the trip with Holbrook while he rented a livery rig and had John Bronson's body stowed in the back carefully wrapped in blankets and canvas. Everyone in Bullhead knew by the following morning what had brought the hill cattlemen to town the previous night. The village was quietly subdued and speculating. Charley Partridge talked endlessly to his customers and wrung his hands.

"Range war," he predicted to all who would listen. "Sure as shootin' it's goin' to end in a range war like they had up in Wyoming."

Gradually too, word passed around that there were phantom gunmen in the Buckskin Hills; secret assassins waiting to kill again. The townsmen agreed among themselves to stay out of the hills, which was perhaps the one good thing to come out of all that loose talk.

When Tim and Grace drove out of town people silently watched. Even after they were well out across the intervening plain between Bullhead and the hills, there were still a number of townsfolk shading their eyes to watch them go.

Grace was quiet. Of all the buggy-rides she'd shared with Tim Holbrook this was certainly the one she least enjoyed. The day was golden and dazzling. Beauty lay on every hand, Nature's lavish display of it overwhelming. Even those northward blue-hazed mountains lay soft-lighted with golden tips.

She clung to the seat when they left the flat country and eased up through the narrow pass, her face pale. But Tim was a careful driver; they got past the worst places without incident. His only comment was that the ranchers ought to spend another few days with their teams and slips scooping out the places where a buggy could scarcely make it through. Grace fervently agreed.

They were half across Stubbs' range when Grace pointed up a hill. A rider sat up there watching them go past. Tim strained to make him out and thought it was Seldon Stubbs because he was lean and supple in the saddle. But whoever he was, the rider just sat up there watching. He made no move to ride down and intercept them. Finally, he turned and loped off his hill heading northward.

"Making for the Bronson place," surmised Tim, letting the team pick their own gait around the sidehills and across the tangle of lifts and rises.

"Will they have already told her?" asked Grace, speaking of John Bronson's wife.

Tim thought on that a moment. "Likely," he admitted. "Old Sam's a tough old nut but he's human. He's got two women on the ranch. The wives of his boys. It'd be like him to send them over there."

"Tim, I hope so. I just don't know what I can do for her."

Tim said nothing. There really wasn't much anyone could do. He'd been through this before, and delivering a dead man to his widow was the most painful part of any lawman's job.

The sun was high before they got within sight of the Bronson place. It wasn't much of a ranch, actually; the house was small and sat upon a little broad bench of flat land where some trees grew and a fresh-water spring ran the year round. A dog was distantly barking from over by the barn and corrals. There was a garden patch with waving stalks of corn in it. Where the wagon road came around the last hill, dipped, then climbed almost straight up to the bench, shade lay silky-soft because of the westward hills.

Tim saw two saddle animals tied out the front at the hitchrack. There was another pair of saddle animals at the rack in front of the barn. When they were close enough to be sure, Tim saw that one of those latter horses was still breathing hard. He made a thoughtful syllepsis: that *had* been Seldon back there watching for them atop the hill. He'd ridden in ahead of them.

Grace put a hand over Tim's arm and squeezed when they came into the yard where tree-shade speckled the dusty earth. He turned and smiled at her. "You'll do just fine," he murmured. "I've yet to see you thrown for a loss, Grace. Besides, you knew her before John married her. You're about the only real friend she'll have."

"Are you going to leave me with her?"

"It'd be best, Grace. I'll let you off then put the rig in the barn."

That's what he did; helped Grace to alight in front

of the house, then climbed back up, turned the team and drove over into the barn. Seldon Stubbs was already in there, sitting morosely on an empty keg whittling with his clasp-knife. He looked up without speaking, snapped his knife closed and got up to come over and lean upon the rig gazing down at the bundle behind the seat.

Tim got down again and went ahead to release each check-rein on the livery team. As he did this he said, "How's she takin' it?"

"Bad," muttered Seldon, turning. "Real bad. My wife came over first thing. Paw sent her. He sent my brother's wife too. 'Said it'd be better if, instead of you just drivin' up with John's body, she was prepared for that, Sheriff."

"Saw you watchin' us from a hilltop back a ways, Seldon."

Young Stubbs threw down the stick he'd been whittling. He hooked both hands in his shell-belt and remained quiet. The yard was as silent as death itself. Sunshine shone through tree leaves with a filtered softness. Tim finished with the horses and walked over to the doorway to lean there gazing over at the house.

Seldon said, "Paw's upset, Sheriff."

Without looking around Tim said, "I reckon."

"He says we should form a big posse an' scour the hills. He also says there's more'n just one of those murderers around."

"That's no secret, Seldon."

Young Stubbs gazed sombrely at Holbrook's back. "Last night you only spoke of one, though."

"Only one shot John Bronson, Seldon."

"If you go nosin' around in the hills, Sheriff, talkin' like that, the other one'll slip up and blow a hole in you." Seldon pushed up off the wagon and walked over to stand with Holbrook in the doorway. Tim turned towards him.

"I doubt it, Seldon. The other one's been in the hills several weeks longer than the one who shot John. He's had time enough to assassinate everyone in here, if that had been his purpose."

Seldon looked surprised. "You knew about these two all along?"

"No. Not all along. I just found out a little about them day before yesterday. But like I just told you, the young one—the feller who's been in the hills longest—isn't a bushwhacker."

"What is he, then?"

"I don't know. He's a feller a little younger than you are. A cowboy from the looks of him."

"Yeah?" muttered Seldon. "I never heard of a cowboy actin' like him, Sheriff. Not a *genuine* cowboy. Killers, yes, but not just every-day rangeriders."

"He's not the one to worry about, Seldon. Did you boys talk to Jim Sargent and Joe Cane on the way home last night about the other one—the one wearin' a black hat and riding a black horse?"

Seldon nodded. "We got a good description of that one, yes. He's the killer, isn't he?"

"I think so."

"Who imported him, Sheriff?"

Tim shrugged. Young Stubbs was a hot-head. Of all old Sam's three sons, Seldon was, Tim Holbrook reflected, probably the most like Sam had been forty, fifty years earlier. But with one very important difference; old Sam's day had been peopled with killers and gunmen. When a man grew to middle life—and survived—it was a safe bet that he'd met and bested his share of gunmen. Seldon never had faced a real killer. If Tim wasn't very careful he was going to give young Seldon all the information he'd need to go hunting one, and that would in all probability, result in Seldon getting killed too.

"I asked who brought this bushwhackin' range detective into the hills, Sheriff?"

"I have no proof," stated Tim evasively. "But even if I did have, it'd be my job, not yours, to do what's got to be done."

Seldon was silent for a while. Over at the house Grace Morgan came out, got something off a chair on the porch and returned to the house again. Aside from that there wasn't a sound anywhere, or any movement either. Birds sang from high in the trees after a while, which was a relief to the quiet men.

Around about stood the ancient hills, fold after rolling fold of them. Distantly visible, like dark spots dropped upon a tawny carpet the colour of mustard, cattle grazed. A few head of horses also showed upon the dun background, some dark, some light. The air was free of the scent of dust which would be noticeable after full summer arrived. By simply moving his eyes a man could see for endless miles in all directions, where the land lifted and buckled, rolling along like some ancient sea frozen in motion.

Tim said, getting away from the topic of the killer, "Did you tell your paw what I said about not holding any more meetings?"

"Yes. He agreed."

That surprised Tim. He hadn't expected old Sam to be that sensible. Then Seldon said why Sam had agreed and Tim's reflections turned saturnine.

"He said we should just ride out lookin' over the

cattle like always, makin' it seem like we accepted John's murder. But at the same time we should concentrate on tryin' our damnedest to figure out where that stock detective was holing up in the hills, an' when we were sure, we'd meet again some late night, then organise our own posse to go after him."

"You fellers won't fool anyone," Tim exclaimed. "That feller's got a spyglass. He can sit in the shadows somewhere an' watch every move you make. Don't you ever believe he won't know what you're doing, Seldon. Knowing things like that is his job. He's stayed alive by being able to second-guess men like you fellers."

Seldon lifted his shoulders and dropped them. "We got to run the risk, Paw says."

Tim growled, "Paw says," in a sarcastic mutter, and turned as the door over at the house opened and Grace walked out again. She came to the edge of the porch and stood there looking barnward.

"She wants you," Seldon observed, and Tim started forward. When he was close enough he could hear the other women inside. They were softly talking to someone, their voices a low sigh of sound. He stopped and Grace gazed at him from her green eyes with a depth of sombreness he'd never seen in her before.

"She wants him buried in the cemetery in Bullhead, Tim. She says it's cleaner there and has green grass."

"Sure, Grace."

"Get the rig and you and I can go back. The Stubbses have agreed to bring her in tomorrow for the funeral. All right?"

He nodded, thinking that this complicated something else he meant to do—stop by the Stubbs' place and raise Cain with Sam for trying to stealthily organise the hill cattlemen in the hunt for John Bronson's killer.

"She's recovering well," Grace said. "The Stubbses had already borne the main brunt of her grief by the time we got here."

"I'm glad of that," he muttered.

"Tim . . .?"

He raised his eyes. She was staring at him. There now seemed to be more to her gravity than just the pain of being with the new widow.

"Yes."

"Are you going after him?"

"Certainly. That's what I'm paid for, Grace."

"Tim. Don't do it alone. Please don't. There's something I've got to tell you. We'll talk about it on the way back. I'll wait over here for you to fetch the team."

He considered her for a puzzled moment, then turned away. At the barn Seldon was already hooking up the horses again. He'd obviously heard what Grace had to say. He handed Tim the lines and helped turn the team without saying a word. As Tim drove out of the barn they nodded at one another, still without speaking.

He drove to the house, helped Grace up, clucked at the team and started back down out of the yard. She rode beside him for a full mile sitting stiff, looking unnatural, then eased back finally, where the road was good, and looked over at him.

CHAPTER EIGHT

"Tim, I don't know how to tell you this. I don't even know how to begin."

He heard the huskiness of her voice and tried to make it easier by saying, "When I was a boy I learnt the only way to get into a cold stream in summertime was to just up and jump in." He smiled. "It's still the best way."

"All right . . . Tim, that young cowboy who's in the hills is my brother."

He drove a hundred yards digesting this. Then he quietly said, "Sure, Grace. I should've figured it was something like that the other night when you kept sayin' he was just a kid passing through. Want to tell me the rest of it?"

"I didn't mean to keep it from you, Tim. That is, I didn't know how to explain it to you. It wouldn't have been so hard if you just hadn't been the sheriff."

He said, "Sheriffs don't eat little babies for breakfast. Every now an' then you'll find one that's a human being."

"I came here from Nevada, Tim. My father and brother and I ranched up there. That was during the Powder River War over in Wyoming. The Wyoming cattlemen had recruiters out hiring cowboys and gunmen to go north and fight settlers."

"Yeah, I know. There were a few of those recruiters down here too."

"Well. But the man they sent to our part of the

country was a tall, cold-eyed man named Idaho Brent."

"I've heard of him," murmured Tim, tooling the rig around a bad corner.

"He killed my father, Tim."

The road straightened for a half-mile before bending around another sidehill. Tim turned and gazed at her without saying anything, then turned back to concentrate on his driving.

"Brent came to our range hiring men. My father called a meeting of the cattlemen. He told them guns weren't going to settle the feuds between grangers and cowmen. He said they should organise and run Brent out of the country. That's what they did. They even got the settlers to join them in it. Brent disappeared just ahead of the posse."

"And he slipped back again," muttered Tim, heading for the lower country near the break in the hills.

"Yes. He came back through the hills. Afterwards, my brother and the others back-tracked him. They even found his hidden camp where he lay in wait for my father. But he was sly, Tim, he knew exactly how to do it. He didn't return for three weeks and by then everyone was certain he'd left the country."

"Naturally, Grace."

"My father and brother were cleaning a waterhole. They had their gun-belts on their saddles and their horses tied to some trees a hundred yards from where they were down on their hands and knees cleaning the little spring when he rode up behind them. My brother said he didn't hear a thing until someone cocked a gun, then he said he tried to whirl around and jump up at the same time, but the ground was muddy and he fell. He saw Brent fire at my father's back. He saw . . . my father try to turn, but the bullet killed him before he

C

could even see Brent. He fell face forward into the mud. Then Brent shot my brother. He didn't come around until that night when the chill of the spring-water brought him around. My father was dead in the mud. Bert had a bullet in his side but the mud had kept it from bleeding too badly."

"So he pulled through."

"Yes. He got home the next day about noon after tying himself on his horse."

They came down out of the hills and had open, flat country before them. Tim hadn't forgotten his desire to go by the Stubbs' place, but this other thing had changed his plans. He looped the lines at the dashboard, fished for his tobacco sack and thoughtfully went to work making a smoke.

Eventually he said, "Was it an accident that you came here, Grace, or did you have some reason for knowing Brent would also come here?"

"Accident or coincidence, whatever you care to call it, Tim. We lost the ranch the following summer. Bert was almost a full year recovering. One day I went to get him and he wasn't there. He'd saddled up in the night and disappeared. I went to Wyoming looking for him. I thought he'd be on Brent's trail and he was. But I never caught up to him. Brent wasn't in Wyoming by then anyway. The Powder River War was over. He'd gone on."

"And your brother Bert followed him down here?"

"Yes."

"And he contacted you?"

"No. He doesn't know even yet that I'm here. The other day when he rode in front of Charley Partridge's store I just happened to be washing my front windows. I almost fainted, Tim, when I saw him out there tying his horse. He'd lost a lot of weight and looked ten years older."

"The hate trail does that to men," murmured Tim, taking the last draw from his cigarette before snuffing it out. "This explains something that's been bothering me about that feller, Grace. I don't know how yet, but your brother knew Brent was coming here to the Bullhead country. Probably, he picked up something farther up the trail; maybe Brent told someone he'd been hired to come down here. Anyway, somehow, Bert arrived in the hills a couple of weeks before Brent did. He's been hiding out, moving his camps, skulking through the hills, trying to find Brent."

"Tim, please find him and stop him."

They were approaching town. Signs of activity were as usual, stirring dust up ahead where ranchers and townsmen drove or rode in and out of Bullhead. It was slightly after mid-day.

"I'll do what I can," he said. "Maybe he'll learn you're here, Grace. If he does—and if he contacts you, I want you to let me know."

She shook her head. "He won't know I'm here. If he's hunting Brent he won't come back to Bullhead until he has to, and by then it may be too late."

"Worrying isn't going to help," Tim told her, steering for the nearest back alley leading into town from the west so that he could leave the wagon at the livery-barn and the body of John Bronson at the doctor's place. "I'll let you out at the barn, Grace."

"Promise me you'll go look for Bert, Tim."

He entered an alleyway and slowed the team. "When I can, I'll hunt for him, but right now I've got to stop something a lot more deadly from happening."

He drew up and handed her down, then drove on

again. At the liverybarn where he halted a man came out, looked in, saw the canvas-wrapped corpse back there and wrinkled his brow. "She wouldn't take her own husband?" that man inquired.

"She wants him buried in the town cemetery," responded Tim, climbing down. "Take him over to the doctor's shed and leave him. We'll have the funeral tomorrow. Ask the doctor to make the arrangements. Now tell me; has Arnold Holfinger ridden out of town today?"

"Not that I know of, Sheriff. At least his horse is still here."

Tim went the rest of the way to his office on foot. When he arrived there Charley Partridge who had evidently been watching from one of his store windows, came rushing over. He burst into Tim's office and said, "Holfinger's Texans are in town." He'd scarcely got that much said when the door opened and Jack Sartain came in. The dark Texan fixed a cold stare upon Partridge until Charley backed around him and retreated out into the yonder afternoon sunlight. Then Sartain closed the door and leaned upon it putting his cold gaze over at Tim Holbrook.

"Too bad about Bronson," he said, as Tim hung up his hat and went to his desk to sit down. "I figured you'd ought to know, Sheriff, didn't I or any of my hands have a cussed thing to do with that."

Tim flicked a glance at Sartain. "Can you say as much for your boss?" he growled, picking up several letters which had been left on the desk during his absence, the morning coach having delivered Bullhead's weekly allotment of mail.

Sartain's answer came slowly. "Sheriff, if I was you I'd calm down a little. That business of you jumpin'

Arnold last night . . . Now that was plumb foolish. After all, you're only one man."

Tim slowly put down his mail and stood up. "Is that a threat," he softly asked, "or a warning?"

Sartain crossed both arms over his chest and continued to lean on the door. His black-eyed gaze turned sardonic. "Well now," he drawled. "I got to change my estimate of you, Holbrook. You're smarter'n I thought. Yeah, it was a warnin'. But I figured you'd be too dense to get it."

Tim moved forward. Instantly Sartain dropped his folded arms. The Texan's black eyes sharpened with quick alertness. He made a long, mirthless smile.

"Don't," he murmured. "What you're thinkin' of tryin', Holbrook—don't."

"Go on back, Jack, and tell Arnold the next time he sends someone down here to threaten me, to at least send a man."

Sartain's eyes narrowed. He straightened up off the door. "I'm man enough," he said. "Any day in the week, tin-badge."

"I doubt that, Jack. Anyone cowardly enough to shoot a steer isn't much of a man."

Sartain's mirthless, long smile, faded. "You callin' me a coward?" he asked.

"Better than that," said Tim Holbrook, ready and waiting. "I just called you a liar, but you were too dense to catch it. You told me yesterday you didn't know anything about Stubbs' shot critter. I know better because the killer was tracked right to your camp. So that makes you a liar."

Sartain gently put his head slightly to one side in a sceptical, assessing manner. "You don't catch me off guard like you did Arnold, lawman," he said softly.

"Your kind I been chewin' up an' spittin' out for twenty years."

Sartain lunged while he was still talking, using the talk to mask his real intention. He walked straight into a blasting short strike that dropped him to his knees and left him looking up stupidly from that position. Tim reached, plucked away the Texan's .45 and stepped back to motion.

"Get up, tough Texan," he said. "Seems to me you need some educating. Get up."

Sartain regained his feet and backed off blinking both eyes. He was still fuzzy-minded; very clearly he wasn't at all sure what had just happened to him. He turned cautious now, moving from side to side, forward and back, on the balls of his feet. He was a seasoned brawler and had the scars to prove it.

Holbrook only moved as was required of him to always keep his face towards the rangeboss. Then Sartain launched himself ahead coming in low. That time Holbrook missed a furious swing and Sartain clipped him lightly as he sped past.

They squared off again, Sartain's confidence and clear-headedness returning rapidly. He caught Tim with a little stinging blow under the jaw. He pawed outward to keep Holbrook off, then sprang at him for the third time. That time Tim didn't miss. He side-stepped because he was expecting the charge, and swung from far down as he turned and leaned inward. The blow sounded like a tree limb cracking. It caught Sartain under the left ear sending him crashing into the desk where he lumpily subsided, his hat rolling away, his feet tangled with Tim's chair.

Holbrook stood a moment flexing his right knuckles. It had been like striking brick. The hand hurt. As the pain subsided Tim went to the door, opened it, went back, raised Sartain up, got under his sodden dead weight, teetered with the rangeboss draped over one shoulder, then scooped up Sartain's hat and gun and walked out into the bright-lighted roadway.

Across the way Charley Partridge gaped in his doorway. Farther up the road other men caught sight of Sheriff Holbrook striding along with Jack Sartain, and also halted to stand with their mouths open.

Holbrook walked all the way up to the *Blue Mule* where several idlers out the front were flabbergasted. He pushed on inside. There weren't many men inside, it was still too early, but Arnold Holfinger was there, standing loose and relaxed at the bar where he was talking with Joe Annakin. Joe's mouth dropped open. Arnold turned slowly, took in the unusual sight, and didn't move a muscle as Tim walked up to him, lowered his shoulder and let Jack Sartain crumple to the floor.

"I told him," Tim said to Holfinger, "to tell you the next time you send someone to threaten me, Arnold, to send a man. But since he won't be able to get that message to you himself, I'm telling you."

The barman leaned far over and looked down at Sartain. He eased back shaking his head in disbelief. But he had no comment to make and in fact, after one glance at the faces of Holbrook and Arnold Holfinger, he prudently stepped clear and went farther along the bar.

"Caught him from behind, eh?" muttered Holfinger, without much conviction in the words.

"Yeah. Like I caught you from behind," growled Tim. "And now, since we're passing out warnings, I've got two for you. The first one is, keep Sartain out of

Bullhead or I'll lock him up. The second is the same warning I gave you last night—keep up this war and you damned well might be the main victim."

Holfinger gripped a whisky glass at the bar while considering his reply. There were only a half-dozen men in the saloon but that was enough. Whatever he said or did now would spread all over town within minutes. "You'd better do a little remembering too," he muttered. "Don't hunt for trouble around me, Holbrook, or you just might find more than you want."

Tim tossed Sartain's hat and gun atop the bar. "Any time," he said. "Any time at all, Arnold." Then he said, "Starting tomorrow any AH riders I find in Bullhead get jailed. And if that's not clear enough, I also include you as one of them."

Holfinger paled. "I warned you," he whispered. "Holbrook, I warned you."

Tim turned on his heel and went as far as the door before turning and saying, "That warning business works both ways. This is what you've been working up to for a long time. All right, Arnold. Now you've got it. Be in town tomorrow and you either get locked up—or shot."

CHAPTER NINE

THE ALTERNATIVES left to a solitary lawman under the kind of circumstances which now prevailed in Tim Holbrook's countryside were simple. He could of course do the customary thing—make up a big posse and go storming through the Buckskin Hills. But although that might look good, he did not delude himself about its effectiveness. Idaho Brent would fade out like he'd done up in Nevada.

The next alternative, and the one Tim Holbrook had decided would be most likely to succeed, was very elemental. He'd moved to implement it when he'd whipped Jack Sartain, then had clinched it by taking Sartain back to Arnold Holfinger where he'd issued his flat challenge to the cowman.

In a few words, what Holbrook had decided was to simply put Holfinger in a position where he'd now concentrate his wrath upon Sheriff Holbrook. That was the best and last alternative Tim had. If he couldn't find Idaho Brent and didn't wish to perhaps get the whole countryside in on his search for Brent, and at the same time still preferred to handle the trouble by himself, then he had to make Holfinger bring the trouble to him. That's exactly what he'd done by confronting Holfinger at the *Blue Mule*. He'd made it mandatory for Holfinger to contact Brent and send the professional killer after Tim Holbrook.

It was dangerous, but also, it was the best way to get his chance at Brent. Finally, it was also the surest method he could think of to keep Grace's brother from tangling with the killer.

Being the bait for Idaho Brent had very little appeal. Brent's notoriety had spread far and wide. There were descriptions of him and endless rumours, but because, as he'd tried to do—and no doubt was certain he'd done—up in Nevada when he sneaked up behind Grace's father and brother, his victims almost always died where he found them, there had never been much to go on for the lawmen who'd chased him.

But Tim Holbrook's scheme, if it worked—and if he survived—would change all that.

He sat in his office smoking and relaxing, and devising methods that might insure his survival. He didn't even look up right away when Grace silently walked in, later in the evening, he was so deep in thought. But when she spoke his name he glanced over at her. Then she said, "The town is buzzing with what happened between you and Holfinger's rangeboss, Tim."

"It'd be buzzing about something anyway," he said, arising to get her a chair.

She motioned the chair away. "I can't stay, I have customers. I just thought you might ride out this evening and I wanted to tell you something before you went."

"Shoot," he murmured, watching her handsome face.

"You may fool the others, Tim, but you don't fool me. You deliberately defied Holfinger and whipped his rangeboss."

"Did I?"

"You certainly did. And I'll tell you why. So Holfinger will concentrate on you and not on anyone else."

He thinly smiled. "What gossip has Charley been peddling this time, Grace?"

"That Holfinger is behind the killing of Charley Bronson."

"I wonder where he got that?"

"He got it from some hill cowmen, Tim. They told him about Brent. Only they didn't know Brent's name. The rest of it I figured out for myself. You're deliberately trying to get Brent to come after you."

Tim crossed to his desk and eased down upon a corner of it steadily eyeing her. "You're not only pretty as spring-time," he said. "You're as smart as an old badger, Grace. All right; let's say you've guessed correctly. What's the alternative? Don't say a posse. It wouldn't work. You should know; it didn't work in Nevada, did it?"

"In a way it did, Tim. At least the posse scared him out of the country."

"No, Grace; because he came back and killed your father and thought he'd killed your brother. A posse is out anyway; I don't want to just scare Brent out of the country. I want him here in Bullhead, dead or alive. I aim to get him that way too. I also want something else—proof that Arnold Holfinger imported him to the Buckskin Hills to bushwhack local cowmen."

"It's too large an order for one man, Tim. You're forgetting that Holfinger has those Texans on his side too. Odds like that almost guarantee your failure."

"The Texans," said Holbrook, "don't worry me right now. Only Brent does that. And as long as we're being frank, you want him kept clear of your brother. Well, if he comes into town tomorrow or maybe tomorrow night to bushwhack me, your brother will still be riding the hills looking for him."

"Tim, I don't want my brother saved at the expense of your life." Grace took two long steps and halted directly in front of Holbrook. "I don't want anything to happen to either of you. That's why I'm begging you to take someone with you. Even one man, Tim. Just a couple of local cowboys even."

He kicked one leg back and forth while studying her face. Then he softly said, "Better get back to the café.

Your customers'll be raisin' Cain if you're not there to keep the coffee cups full."

"Tim . . .?"

He gently shook his head at her. For a moment they stood like that, she pleading with her eyes, he doggedly refusing with his, then she leaned a little, placed both hands upon his chest and brushed his lips with her mouth. After that she whirled and ran out of the office leaving him sitting there on the edge of his desk, but no longer with that dangling leg gently swaying.

Charley Partridge came over after locking up his store for the night. He was almost diffident in the way he eased into the office. Evidently Tim's triumph over Jack Sartain had made a solid impression in some quarters in town.

Charley said, "Sheriff, what I wanted to tell you when I come over here before, was that Holfinger's been talkin' to the town merchants today. He says unless we remove you as lawman there's goin' to be hell to pay and it'll hurt business."

"It might, Charley," remarked Holbrook, standing up. "I don't know exactly how you fellers can remove a duly elected official of the county, but if you decide to try it I won't stand in your way."

"No," exclaimed Partridge. "We talked about it. No one's in favour of knucklin' under to those Texans. But the thing is—will Holfinger make trouble right here in town?"

"I think he might, Charley," said Tim quietly, picking up his hat. "You see, I ordered him out of Bullhead today, an' told him if he or his Texans showed up here again I'd jug 'em."

Partridge blanched. "You didn't," he whispered.

"Tim, for the Lord's sake, that's the same as invitin' trouble."

"Charley, trouble is already here. It arrived yesterday when Holfinger's hired assassin shot and killed John Bronson."

"Holfinger's hired . . .? Tim, are you sure of that?"

"I'm sure enough, Charley. Sure enough to gamble my own neck on it. Now maybe you'd better go on home to supper. One more thing; that young feller who came in and bought those supplies from you a day or so back—he's no killer. He's here to try and get this *real* killer Holfinger has imported."

"You mean he's on our side?"

"Well, Charley, I think it'd be more accurate to say we're on *his* side. Now you'd better drift along. I've got some work to do."

Partridge departed, but he didn't go straight home. He headed unerringly for the *Blue Mule* for a stiff drink first. There were times in a man's life, if he was the worrying kind, when the finest T-bone steak in the world couldn't hold a candle to a straight shot of the greenest whisky. For Charley Partridge, worrier, this was one of those times.

Just before sundown Tim Holbrook sauntered up to the liverybarn. The nighthawk was on duty when he arrived there, and respectfully nodded as Tim walked in.

"Just one question," Tim said. "Is Arnold Holfinger's horse still in its stall?"

"No, sir, Sheriff. About a half hour ago Mister Holfinger got his horse an' rode out."

"Did you happen to see which way he rode?"

"Yes, sir, I did, because he rode out the back way. He went straight across towards the Buckskin Hills.

The same direction them Texans of his rode out earlier."

"Thanks," Tim said, and returned to the roadway. How long would it take for Holfinger to hunt down Idaho Brent? That was the next question. If he knew where to go, not long, but if, as Tim thought more than likely, he had to ride half the night looking and searching, because Brent's kind never let anyone know where they might be in order to keep from ever being sold out by an employer, Holfinger wouldn't make his contact for many hours. Perhaps all night, in fact. In this latter case, Tim Holbrook had a night to relax in before he'd have to start sprouting eyes in the back of his head.

He went across to Grace's place and had supper under her sombre greeny gaze. When she turned pleading he teased her. There were times when Grace's exasperation turned to anger quicker than at other times, but this time it became resigned annoyance because very clearly Tim was not going to change his plans. Later, when he'd finished, Grace walked outside with him. It was a pleasant evening full of stars and soft fragrance. Westerly, the Buckskin Hills were pale tan and ghostly. Northward where the genuine mountains stood, they were darker than the sky and forbidding looking.

Charley Partridge went by with a solemn nod, his shoulders resolutely set, his eyes concentrating with grim attention to keep an even keel as he slightly rolled and heaved through the trough of the night, leaving behind a splendid aroma of whisky.

"His wife'll make him wish he hadn't been born," chuckled Holbrook, and hooked his arm in Grace's arm, leading her southward down through the quiet part of town in a slow walk. "I've been wondering about John Bronson's wife," he said. "Where'll she go; what'll she do?"

"Stay with me for a while," replied Grace. "I've got plenty of room and maybe it'll help, having another woman around. In time she might even start minding the café for me like she used to do. But I suppose, in the end, she'll leave Bullhead. She's young, Tim, and pretty. She can't spend her entire lifetime weeping and moping."

He said, "You're a hard woman, Grace Morgan," teasing her. "I always had a vision of widows wearing long black dresses and weeping at every change of the weather into little scented lace handkerchiefs, and . . ."

"I doubt, Timothy Holbrook, if you'll ever have to worry about a widow. That is of course unless you got married tonight."

He felt the brush of her skirt and the firmness of her arm looped through his. "Tomorrow night'd be better. Or even the night after."

"You're awfully sure of yourself or else you're the biggest fool I've ever known, Tim."

"Some of both, I reckon, Grace."

"Have you always wanted to be a dead hero?"

He grinned. "I've never wanted to be any kind of a hero. But what's the point in getting others involved if it's not necessary?"

"I've told you: it *is* necessary. Brent will shoot, from an alleyway or a rooftop or from between two buildings. He'll waylay you in the liverybarn where it's dark, or he'll wait out on the plain for you to ride out of town. Fighting his kind is like waging war with a phantom, Tim, and no man has enough eyes to watch all the likely places at once."

He stopped at the plankwalk's edge, gazed down the quiet night a moment, then turned and started leading her back again. Finally, just before stepping down into roadway dust where a side-street intervened, he placed both hands at her waist and swayed her in to him. She didn't resist. He kissed her with a gentle passion. She threw herself against him pressing hard and raised up to put both arms around his neck. Then she dropped down, stepped back, turned and resumed pacing northward with her arm hooked in his arm. They didn't speak again until they were almost up to the café. Through the muted sounds of revelry up at the *Blue Mule* she said, "You're not under-estimating him, are you, Tim? After what he's done here, and after what I told you of him in Nevada, that could be the worst error of all."

"No, Grace," he answered. "I'm not under-estimating *either* of them."

She looked quizzical. "Either of them?"

"Brent *or* Holfinger. Arnold left town riding towards the hills. He's not as deadly as Brent, but in his own way he's a lot worse because he brought Brent to the Bullhead country like he's brought other kinds of trouble. Now I'm goin' to turn in and you'd better do the same. Good night, Grace."

"Good night, Tim."

It wasn't much of a walk to the hotel from the café. On the way he passed several cowboys and a brace of townsmen also heading homeward after their nocturnal fun in the saloons. He found himself sizing up each of them long before they got close, and until then he wasn't aware of the strong sense of caution within himself.

Upstairs in his hotel room he stood by the roadside window long enough to have a quiet smoke, gazing out over the town and the westward hills. He had no sense of impending doom nor any particular feelings about his personal destiny. All he thought of was how they would meet, he and Idaho Brent. It didn't occur to him Arnold Holfinger might not have gone after Brent. In fact, if it had occurred to him he wouldn't have heeded such a thought. He did, however, think a moment or two about Holfinger. Whether he got Brent before he himself was shot by Brent or not, Holfinger would still be around, and that, he told himself, was the next thing he had to take care.

He killed the smoke and started shucking his attire. A good night's sleep was the best medicine for anyone under tension, he knew of.

CHAPTER TEN

EARLY THE following morning the mail coach passed through and left some week-old newspapers, but since Bullhead had already received its allotment of letters several days earlier there was no more mail.

At nine o'clock the Stubbses arrived in town with John Bronson's widow. Old Sam was along; his age and general rickety physical condition precluded making the trip very often, but after a stout cup of black java at Grace's place Sam felt renewed, and stiffly hiked over to the jailhouse while his sons and their wives remained with the widow over at the café.

Tim saw the old man coming through his opened roadside door and got up to get him a chair. Sam came in, squinted at the sheriff, and eased down. "Damned wagons they make nowadays with them blasted steel springs can't hold a candle to the old thoroughbrace leather slings for comfort. Tim, I tell you I don't know what this world's comin' too. And idiot'd know steel can't ever replace leather for springs."

They exchanged a long look. Tim said, "How's Mrs. Bronson?"

Sam brushed that aside with a few words, his expression turning bleak. "She's young. She'll pull through." Then he said, "That dirty bushwhacker. When're you goin' to fetch him in so's we can have a hangrope party?"

"I'm waitin' for him now, Sam."

Old Stubbs' bushy brows climbed. "You got a posse out, Tim?"

"No. Last night Holfinger left town. I'm gambling he'll send Brent to Bullhead to bushwhack me."

"Ahhh," sighed the old cowman. "Holfinger. He'd be the one, wouldn't he?"

Tim nodded. "You'll likely see more of him from now on, Sam. I ordered him to stay out of Bullhead. He'll probably live at the cow-camp."

The old man shook his head. "Not if I got him figured right he won't. He'll come back here. His kind can't stand bein' by himself in a cow-camp. He's got to have his liquor and his poker games in town. He's not a real cowman, Tim, he's one of them speculators. As long as cattle prices are good, they stay in the business. When the slumps come, they get into some-thin' else."

Tim agreed with that. He'd often wondered if Holfinger hadn't some time in his chequered past been a professional gambler. One thing was certain, and many local men could verify it, Arnold Holfinger rarely lost at cards. The question now was—would he be as fortunate in other things?

Charley Partridge came in looking wilted. He blinked at sight of Sam Stubbs, surprised at the patriarch of the Stubbs' clan being in town. The old man stiffly nodded.

Tim said mildly, "Care for a drink this morning, Charley?"

Partridge groaned and rolled his eyes. "Why didn't someone stop me last night?" he moaned.

"You're a grown man," said Tim. "How'd your wife take it?"

"You know damned well how she took it," Charley muttered. Then he pushed that unpleasant memory out of his mind and said, "Any word yet?"

"No. But I don't expect they'll send in an advance deputation. You better get on over to the store, Charley."

Partridge nodded and turned to depart. "Take care," he said to the sheriff.

Old Sam sat a moment in thought after Charley had walked out, then heaved himself up out of his chair. "Got to go back to the café," he said, and also departed. Tim went to the doorway and leaned in it gazing up the roadway. Bullhead was beginning to bustle with its usual daily routine. The sun was turning hot, spring-time was rapidly fading before the onslaught of hot summer. Up at the liverybarn the hostler came out and threw a bucketful of water into the road-way to hold down the dust. At the *Blue Mule* several men were leaning upon the hitchrack conversing. Sam Stubbs' two sons appeared on the sidewalk over at Grace's place. They struck out across the road for the liverybarn, walking with purposefulness. A young cow-boy came riding down the roadway from the north, his hair too long as though he'd been a while at some distant cow-camp or line-shack, his clothing rumpled and dusty. He was too far away for Tim to see him good, and before he got into visual range someone hailed Tim from the south roadway. It was one of Hol-finger's Texans. Tim knew the man by sight but not by name. He waited for the rider to come on up and halt out by the hitchrack. The Texan did not dismount. He said, "You got any objections to me pickin' up some stuff we need at the camp from Partridge's store?"

Tim had no objection and said so. Then he asked about Arnold Holfinger. The cowboy gazed across their separating distance, his face impassive, his eyes cautious. "He'll be all right, I reckon, Sheriff. Fellers like Mister Holfinger come out on top." With that veiled threat the Texan reined over across the road, tied up and stepped down. He beat dust from his trousers before entering the store, and at the doorway turned to cast a slow, assessing gaze up and down the roadway.

Tim smiled to himself. The supplies that Texan had come to Bullhead for weren't entirely to be found in Charley's store. He'd been sent to town, the least con-spicuous of Holfinger's tough rangemen, to look the place over and report back. Tim straightened up in his doorway. Well, as the Texan could see, Bullhead was as quiet and unconcerned as always. Holfinger could now send in his killer.

But Bullhead didn't stay quiet and unconcerned.

Tim was up at the liverybarn when it happened, inquiring if any strangers had ridden in and looking into the empty stall where Holfinger's horse usually stood.

The first shot came from the *Blue Mule* across the road. The second one came from the plankwalk just outside the saloon's batwing doors. Tim's initial reaction was to duck and draw, but someone let out a high yell from inside the *Blue Mule*, indicating the firing had come from over there and not from an assassin's gun somewhere close by aimed at the sheriff, so Tim straightened up and started for the roadway.

By the time he stepped out into hot sunlight the sidewalks were both empty. A number of men were peering through store windows but only one or two very bold ones stepped forth to cautiously look left and right.

Arnold Holfinger's Texan was out in the roadway, his drawn gun hanging from a shattered arm, his face contorted with agony. As Tim stepped out the Texan twisted from the middle, dropped his gun in the dust and grabbed for the spreading scarlet stain along his upper arm. He turned a glassy stare on the sheriff as Tim walked over to him.

From over the batwing doors of the saloon the barman's tight-smooth face appeared. When he saw that the Texan was no longer armed he stepped through and called over. "Hey, Sheriff; the other one run out the back way." Even as this was reported Tim heard a horse rush southward down the yonder alleyway towards the far end of town. He started to head back for the liverybarn, then checked himself, went on across to the saloon holstering his .45 as he did so, and the barman went to meet him looking less worried now and more excited.

"It happened almost before I knew it was goin' to," the barman said a little breathlessly. "Good Lord; an' so early in the mornin' too."

"Who was the other one?"

"Never seen him before, Sheriff. Young, nice lookin' feller. Maybe twenty, twenty-two. Needed a haircut an' some clean clothes. He came in a few minutes back, had two beers and ordered the third one. He drank like a feller who'd been a long time between drinks. That other cowboy come in and stepped up to the bar. The shaggy-haired one turned, looked at the other one a minute then he says, 'You're one of those Texans, aren't you?' An' the shot one says he was; that he rode for Arnold Holfinger an' what of it. The shaggy-haired one picked up the third beer—I'd just set it in front of him—walks down the bar to the Texan, and damned if he didn't throw it in his face." The barman rolled his eyes. "I was more surprised than the Texan was. They both went for their guns. That shaggy-haired one was greased-lightnin' fast. I tell you, Sheriff, I don't often size 'em up wrong, but that young buck was far too good with a gun to be just an everyday cowboy. The Texan didn't even have his gun out. But the other one let him have first shot; he just stood there waitin'. The Texan fired an' commenced backin' towards the door. The shaggy-headed feller let him almost make it, then plugged him. Is he hard hit?"

Tim shook his head and turned to gaze out into the roadway where several townsmen were helping the injured man over towards the doctor's house. The barman started talking again, words tumbling past his lips in a stream. Tim wasn't listening. He knew who the shaggy-headed cowboy was—Bert Morgan. The fact that Grace's brother had forced a fight with one of Holfinger's men meant that Bert's long vigil in the hills had shown him who Idaho Brent's employer was. Bert was after more than just Brent, it now seemed like. He left the spouting barman and walked down towards the café. Before he reached it though the local harness-maker and Charley Partridge intercepted him. All he told them was that one of Holfinger's Texans had run into a little trouble up at the *Blue Mule*, and strode on.

Old Sam Stubbs was standing just inside the café doorway with a Winchester in his hands. He eyed Tim warily and returned to watching the roadway. Tim said, "You can put up that iron, Sam, it's all over. One of Holfinger's boys ran afoul of a fast gun up at the saloon." As Tim turned, Grace came from a back room. She halted at sight of Tim. They traded a long solemn look, then he went over to her.

In a low voice he said, "It was your brother. He shot one of Holfinger's riders at the *Blue Mule*."

She said, "No," and moved closer to him. "Are you sure it was Bert, Tim?"

"I'm sure, Grace. I'm also sure of something else, too. He's been spyin' on Holfinger's men. He's some-how discovered they're on Brent's side. He deliberately picked a fight with that Texan, and he deliberately winged him instead of killing him. Grace, I don't like it. Your brother's got no business butting into this thing."

She went to a bench and sat down. He walked over to stand beside her. Old Sam, over at the doorway, re-laxed and put aside his Winchester. As he turned and saw Grace he gruffly said, "Got any more of that black coffee handy?"

She got up. From a rear room came the soft sound of women talking. Sam brushed past Tim as far as the counter and eased down upon the bench over there. He cocked a faded, shrewd eye upwards.

"What was it all about, Sheriff?"

"Just two young bucks, Sam."

"Bantam roosters," growled the old man, planting both skinny elbows atop the counter as Grace brought him his coffee. "In my day a man was careful of his manners an' he didn't go for a gun unless he figured to kill with it. Hmph!"

Tim got as far as the roadside door before Grace caught up to him. She lay a hand upon his arm. "If Bert came to town, Tim, he'd have a reason for exposing himself. I know my brother."

Tim pondered that. "Maybe," he murmured to her, "he knows something at that. Maybe he expected to run into Brent in the saloon, not one of Holfinger's Texans. Grace, I wish he'd kept out of it."

Tim passed out into the roadway, turned and headed for the doctor's house. There, he found the Texan freshly bandaged, pale and shaken, but otherwise alive and ambulatory. Tim went with him across to the tie-rack in front of the *Blue Mule*. Upon the rearward side-walk some curious men stood looking.

"Who was he?" Tim asked the Texan, and got back a tart answer.

"How the hell would I know? Never seen him before in my life. He flung a glass o' beer at me an' went for his gun. I was too danged surprised to do anything for a second." The Texan untied his horse, flung up his reins one-handed, and turned towards Tim. "But I'll tell you one thing; if he ever shows up again I'll be ready for him."

Tim turned the stirrup for the Texan and held it until he'd mounted, using his good hand and arm. As he stepped clear he said, "There had to be a reason, mister."

The Texan denied this. "What reason? I just told you—I never seen him before in my life. He was some shaggy-headed brushpopper from the back-country. The only thing I can figger, Sheriff, is that maybe he's one of them sorehead cowmen from the hills that got a grudge against Mister Holfinger and tried to take it out on me. Outside o' that I got no idea what made him act like he did. But next time by gawd it's goin' to end different."

The Texan hauled his horse around and booted him over into a lope. Tim stood watching him kick up dust on his way out of town. The barman came down beside him, also squinting after the departing rider.

"Damndest thing I ever saw, Sheriff. Wasn't no call for it at all. Them two didn't even know one another, I'd swear to it."

Tim walked around behind the saloon to locate the place where Bert Morgan had tied his horse. He found it, but aside from the imprint of some badly worn horseshoes and some blurred marks made by a man's swiftly moving boots, he didn't come up with anything worthwhile. He hadn't expected to, actually; more than anything else he just wanted to be away by himself while he did a little thinking.

Holfinger's rider would return to the cow-camp and relate what had happened. Unless Arnold, Sartain, and the other men at the camp knew Bert Morgan was in the hills, they'd probably believe as that wounded cowboy believed; that Bert had been one of the back-country cattlemen. If they *did* accept that, then there was an excellent chance they might try to retaliate. Tim swore. Now, his entire plan was upset. Holfinger conceivably would lead his Texans—*and* his killer—against the ranchers instead of concentrating on having Idaho Brent ride to Bullhead.

He called Bert Morgan several uncomplimentary names and struck out for his jailhouse office. He hadn't wanted to have to leave town. Now he'd have to, in order to warn the hill ranchers of what might be building up against them.

CHAPTER ELEVEN

AT THE liverybarn Tim Holbrook told the day-man something to the effect that the best laid plans of men often went to hell in a thimble, and rode out. The day-man scratched his head.

It was a pleasant morning although there was a definite promise of heat later on. As he loped along he remembered they were going to bury John Bronson today. He should've been there. Grace would have expected that. Well, he couldn't be there and that was that. Besides, he'd been to enough funerals in his time. They'd been getting harder and harder to face as the years went by.

He was half across the prairie towards the Buckskin Hills when he saw a rider scuffing dust up a far slope. There was nothing else moving so he watched that man make a big curve and angle down towards the trail far up in the foothills. The rider passed down out of sight into a swale, then popped up again cresting the final roll of hills. He was riding at a loose lope. Tim thought likely he was one of Holfinger's Texans; they ordinarily did their riding after AH cattle along this south-easterly foothill range. He reflected upon that. For all his big talk and tough Texans, Arnold Holfinger was still just barely hanging on in the Buckskin Hills. One good drive by the established cowmen back in there would drive him out of the hills and down onto the plain.

Of course he'd go right back in, and furthermore, up until now at any rate, all the back-country ranchers had done was mutter, and occasionally push the AH critters away when they penetrated too deeply into another cowman's domain.

As a matter of fact, Tim thought, still watching that horseman, if Holfinger hadn't pushed so hard the chances had been excellent that in time the hill folk would have accepted his right to be there among them. The trouble with that was simply Arnold Holfinger: He was not a man who could abide peacefulness. There always had to be some action in prospect even if it was only a poker game or a drinking contest. That kind of a man, given half a chance, was always trouble, sooner or later.

The rider dropped down a deer run and hit the main trail leading out of the hills. Tim Holbrook was coming up the same trail. They met near the mouth of the canyon in a wall of thin shade. The other man was Seldon Stubbs. He said, "I was ridin' to fetch you, Sheriff. We got some trouble back at Jim Sargent's place."

"Is that so," stated Tim. "When did you leave town, Seldon?"

"Right after we ate breakfast at Miss Grace's place. Paw sent me'n my brother out."

"Out where?"

"To pass the word among the ranchers Holfinger was behind the murder of John Bronson, and to fetch them back to town to stand with you against this Brent feller who they say is a professional bushwhacker."

Tim pursed his lips remembering how old Sam had listened when Charley Partridge had visited his office first thing, hours before, and also how Sam had abruptly left the office after Charley had. It wasn't hard to figure out where Sam's suspicions had led him. Nor was it hard, knowing Charley as Tim Holbrook did, to figure out what Charley had told him.

"I'm obliged to your paw," Holbrook told young Stubbs, "but I don't need the ranchers to stand with me. Now about this trouble . . ."

"Someone shot a horse out from under Jim Sargent, Sheriff, an' to hear him tell it if Joe Cane hadn't happened along that same bushwhacker would have finished Jim off."

"Why didn't they ride to town with you?"

"Jim's hip is dislocated. He can't stand, let alone straddle a horse. He and Joe are holed up at Sargent's cabin waiting for that bushwhacker to try again." Seldon began nodding. "It's that Brent, I'll bet you a new hat."

"You'd lose," stated Holbrook drily. "If it'd been Brent Jim would be dead." He thought a moment then said, "Seldon, I want you to ride to the Spanglers' place and spread the word for the ranchers to hole up.

Go among all the ranches and say the same thing—
hole up and keep close watch for attackers. Tell the
menfolk to keep their kids and women inside."

"Brent again, Sheriff?"

"No. At least if Brent's along he won't be the only
one. Holfinger's Texans. One of them got shot in town
this morning. I have a feeling Holfinger is going to
think the man who did that to his cowboy was one of
the back-country cattlemen."

"Well, who was he?"

Tim said, "Never mind that for now. You just make
the rounds. And be damned careful while you're doing
it."

Seldon lifted his reins. "I'll be careful all right,
Sheriff. You should've seen me comin' this far from
the Sargent place. No danged redskin was ever so sus-
picious of shadows." Seldon tightly grinned. "You
headin' back for town now?"

Tim nodded. "Directly," he said. "Why?"

"Tell paw what I'm up to."

"Sure," agreed Holbrook, and turned his mount.

They separated at the pass, Seldon riding north-
westerly through a long swale, Tim Holbrook easing
his horse off in a different direction and skirting the
big swell directly in front of him. He'd had a thought
while sitting back there conversing with young Stubbs:
if Holfinger was throwing his range crew into his fight
with Holbrook and the hill country ranchers, they
wouldn't be at their cow-camp. He wanted to ascer-
tain this for a fact.

What made him believe this was happening was the
way Jim Sargent had been brought down. Idaho Brent
wouldn't have been that clumsy. No professional killer
would have, particularly when he had a telescope to

pick up his target with. That shooting struck Holbrook as both hasty and amateurish; the work of a willing but inexperienced assassin.

As he worked his way carefully through the hills he regretted not arresting Holfinger the day before instead of just running him out of Bullhead. But at that time he'd had a different plan, one that involved having Holfinger loose to contact Idaho Brent.

He eventually came to a worn saddlehorse trail leading upwards to a plateau. Here, he rummaged around for a good place to leave his horse hidden, then went the balance of the way on foot carrying his carbine.

It was hot and breathless. He stopped often to catch his breath and came up from underneath the cow-camp plateau where there were no trails, making discovery less probable. When he got within ten yards of the hilltop he stopped for the last time, listening. There wasn't a sound up there. Emboldened by this he covered the final few yards, got belly-down and poked his head over the last rise.

The camp was as rumpled and disorderly as it had been the time of Holbrook's previous visit. The old wagon stood forlornly alone up there with bright sunlight touching it. There was not a man nor a horse at the camp. Holbrook got up, dusted off and walked on in. He approached the wagon from the rear, pulled aside the tailgate canvas and peered in. It was empty. He moved here and there reading sign and gathering impressions.

The number of fresh tracks showed that eight men had ridden westerly not long before. That was the direction of Jim Sargent's place. It was also the general direction of the other ranches. Holbrook speculated; Seldon would probably elude Holfinger's crew because, being alert now, he'd spot the dust raised by eight horsemen. But what Holfinger was up to troubled Holbrook more than any possible meeting between his crew and young Stubbs.

It seemed that Holbrook's first thoughts back in town were correct: Holfinger was going to strike back over what he thought had been an attack upon one of his men by the hill men. Yet now it seemed likely Holfinger wasn't riding to the attack so much as he was heading for some rendezvous. The Stubbses were Holfinger's mortal enemies, and yet he wasn't swinging southward towards their place at all. It was possible he knew they weren't at the ranch; perhaps his wounded rider had seen them in town. But Holbrook's feeling of puzzlement persisted, so he changed his own plans. Instead of returning directly to town he went back to his horse, got astride, and quartered around until he picked up the trail left by Holfinger's crew, and followed it.

The farther he went the more positive he became that Holfinger wasn't heading for any of the nearby ranches at all. Not for a solid hour, or until he was bending around in the direction of the Sargent place, which was one of the farthest ranches, did it occur to Holbrook that Holfinger was heading for some particular rendezvous. Then it struck him.

Holfinger was juncturing with Idaho Brent!

He came across a round rise and upon its farthest slope sighted the Sargent place down in its broad little valley surrounded by naked slopes. Here though, Holfinger's trail veered sharply southward. He had, Holbrook speculated, gone far out and around so as not to be seen from the Sargent ranch. Westerly, farther back, the hills became more wild and tangled; an ideal place for Idaho Brent to have his base-camp because seldom did anyone ride over in there.

Holbrook set his horse down the first trail he encountered heading straight for the Sargent place. Long before he reached the yard he sighted the cold reflection of sunlight off a gun-barrel poked through a window. Either Jim or Joe Cane had been keeping watch. He walked his mount around the last bend in the trail and emerged into the barnyard. Coming on around into the open yard beyond he saw a second gun trained on him. He called out from the centre of the yard, halted and sat his saddle until the men inside the cabin were satisfied. It wasn't a very long wait. Joe Cane came out with his carbine held upwards in front of his body in both hands. He squinted from the porch.

"We weren't exactly expectin' you, Sheriff," Joe said. "Put your horse in the barn an' come on in."

Holbrook swung down, nodded up at Joe and led his horse over into the pleasant shade of Jim Sargent's barn. Just from force of habit he tugged out his Winchester and started across the yard carrying the weapon. Joe was waiting for him over there on the porch, swinging his head left and right as he waited. When Holbrook came on up Joe said, "Someone killed Jim's horse under him. He stove up his hip in the fall. He's inside." Joe preceded Holbrook into the little cabin.

Bleak-eyed Jim Sargent gazed up from a cot over against the back wall where he'd propped himself with a pistol and a carbine at his side. "Howdy, Sheriff," he said. " 'Joe tell you someone knocked a horse out from under me?"

"Seldon Stubbs told me first," said Holbrook, walking closer to the injured man. "How bad is it?"

"Bad enough," growled the injured man. "Just now when Joe seen you top out on the hills I hobbled to a window, and it hurt plenty. But nothing's broke, I don't expect. I landed like one of them dancers doin' the splits, all my weight on the right side. Popped the ball an' socket joint I reckon. It's back in place now, but I've felt a sight better in my time."

"Who did it, Jim?" Holbrook asked.

"Damned if I know, Sheriff. One minute I was ridin' down that same trail you come into the yard on, and the next moment someone commenced firin' at me. I run my horse straight for the house. He caught me short of the yard where I tried to confuse him by swingin' wide and comin' uphill from behind the house."

"More than one shot?" asked Holbrook.

"Hell yes; he emptied his Winchester before he connected. There was dust flyin' all around me. He was downhill an' across the gulch in that tall grass beside the trail." Sargent squinted upwards. "You reckon it was this stock detective Seldon says folks are accusin' of killin' John Bronson?"

Holbrook shook his head. "Think it over, Jim. The stock detective picked Bronson off over a hundred yards away in the last daylight, an' he fired just once to nail his man."

Joe Cane turned from rummaging a cupboard. He had a half-bottle of rye whisky in one big fist. " 'Never thought o' that," he muttered. "By golly, Sheriff, I believe you're right."

"Then who?" demanded Sargent.

Holbrook said, "Maybe one of Arnold Holfinger's men. Who else would want to bushwhack you, Jim?"

"Well hell, why would they? Oh, I admit we got no

D

love between us, but I've never gone out of my way to . . ."

"Because, boys," said Holbrook, "a young cowboy shot one of Holfinger's Texans in town this morning, and I've a strong hunch he thinks it was one of the hill ranchers who did that."

Jim Sargent reached for the whisky bottle and took a hard pull at it. He made a frightful grimace and offered Holbrook the bottle. Tim refused so Jim handed the bottle back to Joe Cane. Joe also took a hard pull, corked the bottle and set it aside. He didn't bat an eye.

It was hot inside the little cabin. Holbrook crossed to the door and opened it. That didn't help much because there wasn't a breath of air stirring outside.

"Well," Sargent asked grumpily, "what do we do, Sheriff; just sit around here waitin'?"

"For a while," Holbrook said, standing loosely in the doorway. "Then we'll load you into your wagon, hitch the team, and Joe can drive while I out-ride ahead just in case . . ."

Holbrook stopped speaking. He slowly drew up off the doorjamb staring far out. From his bed Sargent asked what was wrong. Holbrook didn't reply. Joe strode over and also peered out. Eventually he said, "Be damned, Jim. There's another rider comin'."

Tim lifted an arm and pointed farther back beyond the approaching horseman, who was rapidly heading for the ranch. "Not just one, Joe. Look farther back there. A whole line of 'em chasing that rider."

Joe looked and mumbled something. From his cot Jim Sargent cursed and eased around to try and arise.

They all heard the waspish, distant echo of gunshots. Those farthest riders were shooting at the man racing for the Sargent place. Tim Holbrook grabbed up his carbine and ordered the others to do the same. "I don't know who he is, boys, but he sure needs some help. Get to the windows and give him cover when he gets into the yard."

CHAPTER TWELVE

THE RACING rider came down the far slope without even attempting to use the trail. It was a wild and reckless thing to do but he had no other choice, and whether his mount went end over end or not, if he turned careful now, with that hurtling band of hard-riding pursuers back there firing at him, he wasn't going to make it anyway.

Tim watched with held breath. Jim Sargent, using a chair as support, got to a window and looked out. "Lord," he exclaimed, forgetting his personal agony as he watched. "He'll never make it."

The pursuing horsemen swept along the top of the same hill firing downwards. Holbrook, who'd done that kind of shooting himself a time or two, knew how inaccurate it could be. "If the horse doesn't go down he'll make it," Tim said.

The horse didn't fall, but it was sheerest luck that he didn't. When his rider eased him down to a slower gait near the bottom of the draw the horse put his head down and forward, at last picking his footing with care.

Uphill, those horsemen—nine of them—threw more

lead. One rider dismounted, tugged out his Winchester, walked deliberately along the rim until he found a suitable place, and dropped to one knee. Tim Holbrook watched that man intently. He knew exactly what he was about; he was also as cold as ice about doing it. Tim had never seen Idaho Brent but he was certain he was now looking at the notorious murderer.

"Throw a little lead up there," he called to Joe Cane and Sargent. "I know the range is too great but divert that kneeling man if you can."

Jim and Joe obediently pushed out their Winchesters and took elevated aim. Meanwhile, the fleeing man had got across the draw and boosted his horse straight up the near side towards the yard. When Joe and Jim fired, the pursued man threw up his head in quick consternation. Tim stepped over to the door and shouted.

"Zig-zag! Zig-zag!"

The cowboy heard and understood. He hauled his horse sharply to the left as the beast hunched up trying to jump along up the hill. Joe and Jim levered and fired again. Up the far slope that kneeling man didn't fire. He tracked his prey with his carbine but did not fire. Although the other men up there were distracted by the firing from Sargent's cabin, that kneeling man only lifted his head once, looked across, then ignored the shooting. He was, Tim thought, the coolest man under fire Holbrook had ever seen.

Finally, the fleeing man ducked over into the protection of Sargent's barn, and halted his heaving horse. He was out of range. Also, he was behind a large building. He'd made it.

Joe gave a little triumphant whoop and fired off his third shot up the hill. Tim stepped back, put his carbine aside and kept watching the pursuers. "Holfinger and his Texans," he said.

Joe Cane strained to make that identification and failed. "You got better eyes than I have, Sheriff. Where'd that other feller go?"

"Into the barn from around back," said Sargent. "If that's Seldon he sure can ride a sight better'n I ever figured he could. Hey, Sheriff, hadn't we better go down there an' help him?"

Tim dropped his attention from those nine men up the distant slope long enough to say, "No; he's safe enough for now. But we might not be. Look up the hill."

The dismounted gunman up there had arisen, gone back and mounted up. He gestured with his rifle for the others to follow him, turned and headed straight for the trail leading down to the Sargent place. The others lined out behind him without a dissenting gesture.

"Well, well," muttered tough Joe Cane coolly. "Maybe that bucko in the barn can return us the favour of helpin' him, Sheriff. Looks like we're about to get attacked."

There was no question about that, but what was holding Sheriff Holbrook's immediate attention was that stranger over in the barn. The others might believe he was Seldon Stubbs but Holbrook knew better. In his trade a man trained himself to be observant; Seldon, when he and Holbrook had met at the pass, had been riding a bay horse and wearing a grey work shirt. He'd had a good look at the stranger when he yelled at him to zig-zag; he was riding a sorrel horse and was wearing a blue shirt.

"Here he comes," said Joe from his vantage place at

a window. "Must've been puttin' up his horse at the barn."

Holbrook, still standing in the open doorway, swung for a look. The young stranger was coming towards the cabin at a trot. He had his carbine in one hand and several small cardboard boxes in the other hand. He had evidently watched those armed men riding towards the downward trail and had also accepted the probability of another hard fight. He was shaggy and rumpled looking.

"Damned if I ever seen this one before," muttered Joe, drawing his brows downward and inward. " 'You, Jim?"

"Nope. Plumb stranger to me. How about you, Sheriff?"

"His name's Bert," said Tim, stepping aside as the trotting man sprang up onto the porch. "Bert Morgan. He's the one who shot Holfinger's rider in town this morning. They must have spotted him passin' through the hills. Maybe the feller he winged recognised him. Otherwise I don't think they'd have tried so hard to nail him."

Young Bert Morgan came through the door in a wide-eyed rush, then halted, gazing around. He looked longest at Tim Holbrook's badge. For a moment no one spoke, then young Morgan bobbed his head brusquely.

"Thanks, fellers," he said. "When you first opened up I thought sure I was between two fires and done for. I'm right obliged to you."

Joe and Jim wordlessly regarded the younger man. He looked half wild and shaggy as a sheep dog. Tim Holbrook said. "The feller leaning on the chair is Jim Sargent. The feller at the window is Joe Cane. I'm Sheriff Tim Holbrook from Bullhead. You're Bert

Morgan, late of Nevada—but by way of Wyoming and a few other places."

Young Morgan's bright, hard eyes became totally still. After another long moment of appraising Holbrook he said, "You're good at your job, Sheriff. How long have you known?"

"Not long, Bert. Your sister told me."

That seemed to shake Bert Morgan. "My sister . . .? You mean, Grace?"

"Yes. She runs a café—in Bullhead."

Morgan's eyes got round. "My sister—runs a café —in Bullhead?"

"Yes. The other day when you rode in to buy supplies, she recognised you. We're sort of good friends. She told me who you were. But before that I knew you were in the hills. What I *didn't* know until she told me, was *why* you were here."

Morgan gradually recovered from his astonishment. He looked at Cane, at Sargent, then back at Holbrook again. "Mind tellin' me," he asked softly, "why I'm here, Sheriff?"

"Because Idaho Brent is also here."

Morgan nodded. "Bull's-eye," he said. "You fool a man, Sheriff, damned if you don't."

"Hey," said Joe Cane. "Where'd they jump you?"

Bert Morgan slowly turned towards Cane. "Westerly a few miles. I've been hunting high an' low for Brent's camp. I found it, finally, last night, when he made a little cookin' fire. I lay atop a hill overlookin' the camp all night with my guns, just waiting. Then, when Brent left his shelter to go after his hobbled horse, I stalked him. Luckily, I'd hid my horse in a gulch. When those riders showed up I don't know who was most surprised, me or them. Anyway, they hollered to Brent and he ducked into some trees. I tried a shot anyway, but it only knocked bark off Brent's tree. Then I had to run for it and ride like hell. They came after me like a herd of redskins.

"I remembered this cabin. It was my only chance, it bein' the nearest cover, so I made for it. You know the rest of the story."

Joe stepped back to his window and took a long look outwards. "It's not finished yet," he said. "They're comin' over behind the barn." He looked back and grinned. "Much obliged, Morgan," he said, "it's been damned dull around here today." He checked his Winchester and moved closer to the window.

Jim Sargent pushed his chair closer to the front wall also. He used it to prop his injured leg against as he shoved his carbine through another window. "Sort of whittles down the odds, havin' you in here too, Morgan. By the way, if you're dry there's a bottle of rye whisky over by the cot."

Tim Holbrook eased up to the door, closed it part way and peered out. There was a little dust lazily stirring over by the barn but aside from that he could see nothing because the barn was between the house and their attackers.

Joe Cane soberly said, "Jim, next time you build a barn please put it somewhere else."

Jim chuckled. Those two were hard, fearless men. Bert Morgan's pale gaze brightened a little as he watched and listened to them. He moved over beside Holbrook and said, "Good spot I picked, Sheriff. But I'm sorry I had to drag you boys into my fight."

"Not your fight exclusively, Bert," replied Holbrook succinctly. "Jim, the one with the bad leg—he ran afoul of the same men hours before you did. At least he ran afoul of *one* of them, but fortunately it wasn't Brent. Otherwise he'd be dead now instead of just crippled."

Bert craned for a look out into the silent, empty yard. It was the lull before the storm. He turned back toward Holbrook and asked a question: "Who's the fancy-dan leadin' those Texans? Up until yesterday I thought I'd memorised every man in that cow-camp. But this big dude in the frock coat's a new one."

"That's Arnold Holfinger, the boss of the Texans. The reason you haven't run into him before is because he spent all his time in town, until I ordered him out of Bullhead yesterday. But don't let that coat or that ruffled shirt fool you. He's the worst of the lot. He's the one who brought Brent to this country."

Bert bent to check the loads of his carbine. As he did this he put the little boxes he was holding to one side. They were bullet containers. "In that case," he murmured, "I reckon next to Idaho Brent, Mister Holfinger's my next enemy."

The silence ended several moments later when someone hailed the cabin from the barn. At first, because the voice was muffled by the barn, Holbrook did not recognise it. But before it was through calling he did. Arnold Holfinger was in Sargent's barn. If any of them had ever had doubts about the identity of their attackers, that voice erased them all.

"Hey, Holbrook," Holfinger sang out. "I know you're in there. We've got your horse here in the barn. Send that feller out who just rode in on this sorrel horse."

Tim leaned in the cracked doorway looking and not bothering to answer. Joe Cane swore heavily, grimly, and snugged back his carbine, waiting for the shot he wanted.

"Holbrook, send that feller out here and we'll leave you in there with your crippled friend."

Joe raised his head and looked at the others. Jim, too, looked around. They were all thinking the identical thought. How would Holfinger have known Sargent had been hurt unless he also knew who had tried to ambush Sargent?

"Well," drawled Jim Sargent, "I reckon that clinches the question of who tried to bushwhack me, don't it?"

"Sure does," replied Cane. "An' how come them not to know I'm in here too?"

Jim said, "Joe, did you turn your horse out?"

"No. He's in a stall too. But I unsaddled him."

"Then they figure he's just another of my horses," suggested Sargent, and smiled. "They're in for a surprise, aren't they?"

Holfinger cried out again. "Holbrook, quit playin' possum. We know you're in there with Sargent and that punk who tried to shoot one of my men a while back. If you'n Sargent want to stay alive send that punk out here."

Finally, Tim Holbrook answered. "Arnold, last night I whipped the wrong man. That was my mistake. But I won't make the same mistake again, and if you're just half smart you won't try fightin' your way in here."

Jack Sartain's gravelly voice rang out next, full of anger and hatred. "Hey, Holbrook, you're goin' to die today. How's that set with you?"

"Ask an hour from now," replied Tim. "Sartain, if you can't shoot any better'n you dog-fight, you'd better get on your horse and leave right now."

Sartain roared back a string of fierce curses, and someone down there in the barn, either Jack Sartain or someone else, fired a .45 at the house. Where the slug struck wood splintered. At once Joe Cane's carbine roared and bucked. Joe stepped back, levered up his next bullet and peered down towards the barn.

No second shot came from down there though. The silence returned. Inside Sargent's house the men sweated. There wasn't a breath of air stirring; sunlight beat unmercifully downward. Over at the barn a thin spindrift of dirty grey gunsmoke drifted out of the doorless opening in the heavy atmosphere.

Jim Sargent said, "There's water in the drinkin' bucket if anyone's thirsty." Then he said, "Or whisky in the bottle."

Tim eased the door closed and bolted it. He and Bert Morgan exchanged a look, neither of them saying a word. Bert crossed over to the window where Jim was, and Tim turned to cross the room towards the cot. There was a rear window there too, but much smaller and higher in the wall than the front windows.

"They're up to something," Sargent finally growled, as the silence ran on unbroken. "Sheriff, you keepin' a watch around the back?"

Tim said he was, and leaned against the rear wall peering outward. The stillness piled up. It made the defenders uneasy. Holbrook had never under-estimated Arnold Holfinger's craftiness. He did not under-estimate it now.

CHAPTER THIRTEEN

"HEY!" CALLED Jim Sargent from across the room. "Look yonder up the westward hill where Holfinger's crew was a while back."

There was an urgency to Sargent's tone that brought Holbrook swiftly back to the front of the cabin. Joe Cane and Bert Morgan also craned around to look westward.

"Who the devil is that?" Joe asked.

There were three riders sitting their horses up there watching the Sargent ranchyard. Tim strained to identify those motionless figures and failed. As he turned Sargent said he didn't see how it could be any more Texans because Holfinger's entire crew, plus one additional man, was already in the yard.

Bert Morgan leaned for a better look and a gunshot erupted. Wood flew, a sharp splinter struck young Morgan making him stagger back, and Joe Cane immediately roared a defiant curse and shot back. Other guns opened up from the barn. The defenders returned this brisk fire hotly. Bert Morgan's bleeding cheek made him look badly injured while actually he had nothing more than a deep scratch. But the wound also seemed to anger Morgan. He pumped lead into the barn almost without aiming, or at least it appeared that way.

Holfinger's rangemen were firing from the front as well as the rear of the barn. Holbrook, trying to get one of the men out the back who had to jump forth exposing themselves to fire accurately, then jump back again, thought it odd that most of the Texans should be at the rear of the barn. He also thought it very probable, until the firing had been resumed, that Holfinger had sent those men back there to be ready to make a rush on the cabin. He worked hard at letting them know, if a rush had been their intention, it would be very costly. He seemed to succeed for those riders around the back became less and less anxious to jump out, fire, and jump back again. Holbrook hadn't hit one, he was sure of that, but his fast answering shots had inspired considerable caution.

None of them had any more time to ponder over those three horsemen up the westerly slope until the fighting dwindled again, some two minutes later, and by then the three riders were gone.

"Strays passin' through," muttered Jim Sargent. "Every now an' then I see riders up there. Those westerly hills aren't inhabited and even the stock don't drift over into them very much. It makes a good place for drifters to lie over for a few days."

Joe Cane had something to add to that. "Not only drifters, Jim. I've spied a few back there that've made quite a point of not wantin' to be seen."

Bert Morgan said, "It's a big country back in there. I rode up an' down it for almost two weeks lookin' for Brent's camp. Big and rough."

"Well anyway," summarised Joe Cane, "whoever they were, they're gone now, and can't exactly say as I blame 'em. The odds down here might seem a little one-sided."

Tim Holbrook kept watching the back of the barn. If they could prevent Holfinger's men from leaving the barn, they wouldn't have to worry about the back of the house. He said as much to the others.

The lull was longer this time. Tim thought he understood why that was. Instead of facing just Morgan, Sargent and Holbrook, the Texans had discovered there was still another gun in the cabin, and a fast-firing one at that. They would eventually accept this, though, Holbrook thought, because the odds and firepower still lay with Arnold Holfinger.

Bert Morgan settled close to a shattered window and kept vigil. The barn had more dirty smoke drifting out of it but there wasn't a man in sight down there. As before, the silence became more oppressively leaden than the gunfire had been.

Tim crossed the room to look out the little rear window. At once he saw three men crawling forward through the grass on their stomachs. He flung up his carbine, halted and stared hard at a grey shirt on a slim frame off to the left. He'd seen that shirt earlier and instantly recognised both it and the man inside it.

"Help's coming," he called over one shoulder. "Seldon is out in back creeping up with Ariel and Clay Spangler. That's who it must have been on the hilltop a while back."

Joe Crane and Bert Morgan rushed over to shoulder Tim aside for a look. Sargent made slower progress. Just as he reached the back window the gunfire started up again from the barn.

Tim sprang back to the front wall and flattened there listening to a harsh spray of lead along the front wall. He had no more time for other things for a full three minutes.

The battle brisked up, became general and intensely fierce; more fierce than it had been up to now. Joe, Jim, Bert Morgan, came back to the front of the building to swap shots, but as before, because the defenders as well as the attackers were too well protected, the duel ended in a draw. Not before Holfinger cried loudly to his men that he'd give a thousand dollars for Tim Holbrook's punctured hide, and had, for this offer, drawn a violent volley of gunfire from the house that drove his men completely away from the front of the barn. After that, with gunfire diminishing down at the barn, the defenders also slackened their fire. Jim Sargent flung sweat off a red face and said, "Joe, go open the back door an' let them fellers in. I'd do it but my leg's troublin' me."

Cane turned and walked through a doorless doorway into a tiny kitchen-pantry combination. The firing had stopped again, enabling the others in the front room to hear Cane opening a door. They heard him whistle. Moments later there was a rush of booted feet over hard ground and the solid stamp of men coming into the pantry from out the back, murmuring quickly as they ducked past Joe and headed for the parlour.

Holbrook eyed young Seldon Stubbs first, then the Spangler brothers. "Thought you fellers were going to look out for the women and kids, and stay holed up," he said.

Seldon shrugged and looked around the room where brass cartridge casings brightly shone around the floor. "We talked it over and decided we'd come get Joe and Jim, then fort up at my home place, Sheriff. But when we heard the gunshots we sort of changed our plans." Seldon tentatively grinned. "Oh, we still aim to take Jim and Joe back with us, but first we got to thin out a pack o' skunks it looks like."

The big Spangler brothers were stolidly examining Bert Morgan. Clay, the youngest, finally said, "Sheriff, this here feller looks a heap like that stranger we told you was leavin' little camps around on our range."

Tim introduced the men but had time for nothing more. Arnold Holfinger was calling again from within the barn. "Hey, Holbrook; you had enough yet? Listen to me now; we're giving you your last chance. Send out that feller who rode in on the sorrel, and the rest of you can stay here while we ride off with him."

Tim called back. "Arnold, he didn't hit anyone, he only tried. Why do you want him so badly?"

"Never mind that," answered Holfinger. "I just want him. Send him out."

Tim thought a moment, then said, "Suppose he's dead, Arnold; you still want him?"

"In that case, Holbrook, roll him outside where we can be sure."

Tim turned towards Morgan. "Like I thought," he said. "Holfinger doesn't know you. He'd have no reason to keep up this fight—unless . . ."

"Unless?" asked Morgan.

"Well, you just heard him. He doesn't care whether you're alive or dead but he wants to make sure. In other words, Bert, it's not Holfinger who's dead set on getting you dead, it's someone else."

"Brent," exclaimed Bert Morgan. "He must've recognised me when I tried to shoot him. Or maybe when I had to run across open country to get back to my horse. Sure, Sheriff; if Brent recognised me he wouldn't rest until he finished me off like he thought he'd done up in Nevada."

The others looked and listened, not comprehending any of this. Holbrook turned back and called down towards the barn again. "Hey, Arnold; you're paying

Brent, that ought to be enough. You shouldn't have to fight his battles for him too."

During this brief exchange one of the attackers had used the diversion to creep stealthily along the rear of the barn on his stomach until he lay now at the extreme corner of the building with his carbine trained upon the house. He fired just as Sheriff Holbrook finished speaking and stepped back to raise his Winchester. The bullet knifed through flimsy window siding, cut Holbrook's sleeve at the shoulder, passed directly between Seldon Stubbs and big Ariel Spangler, and struck the back wall with shuddering impact.

Tim sprang away and gazed at his torn shirt. Young Stubbs and Ariel Spangler turned angry and advanced upon the front windows. Clay also strode forward. By the time Holbrook got back over there also, there was hardly room enough for another man. They all poured a savage fire at the juncture of the barn's rear and side wall. Splinters flew, dirt leapt up in clods, gunfire thundered and deafeningly echoed, and for nearly a full sixty seconds the volleys did not cease.

At the barn the men with Arnold Holfinger seemed stunned. A few tried half-heartedly to return the gunfire, but after several near hits, they retreated, leaving both the front and rear openings unmanned.

"Pour it in," growled angered Ariel Spangler. "Give 'em what for, consarn 'em!"

The men tore off lengths of barn siding. They wrecked the framework around the front doorway. They drove lead in a wild stream straight through the walls. Jim Sargent's small house fairly shook on its fir-log foundation with reverberations.

Finally, Holbrook shouted over the tumult for his defenders to hold their fire. Reluctantly, they did, dropping only an occasional shot after a while, and eventually stopping even that.

From over at the barn there wasn't a sound. Holbrook went to the water bucket, drank a dipperful and wiped off sweat. He made a wry grin at the others. What had started out as a fight with all the advantage on Holfinger's side, had gradually turned into something altogether different. He could imagine Arnold down there in the barn trying to placate his shaken men, and at the same time trying to explain to himself what had happened. Where there had originally been only four riflemen facing him—and he'd only belatedly discovered there *was* a fourth one—now there were seven guns pouring lead like water into his improvised fortress. Whatever earlier prospects for triumph he'd had, he now could not have. And if he'd once entertained hopes of rushing the cabin, he now could not but help realise the deadly futility of such an idea.

Jim Sargent hobbled back to his cot and gingerly sat down. He started plugging fresh loads into his Winchester. After a while he looked up from a pained face and said, "Say, Sheriff, how about me makin' Holfinger and them Texans of his fix my barn when this is over? Holy mackerel; 'you see how we done wrecked it?"

Joe Cane laughed, then said, "Jim, if this doesn't end right you're not goin' to need a barn anyway."

The other men were also amused. It tended to relax them. They came over to drink water and wipe off sweat. The yonder yard was as still as a tomb. Sunshine brightly burned out there, and a cloud of soiled gunsmoke hung in the hush, but otherwise there was nothing to indicate rival fighting factions were holed up in the house and the barn.

Finally, as Tim Holbrook went back across the room to look out, they all heard a horse snort down at the barn. It was that still. Holbrook instantly straightened up and looked around the edge of a ruined sill. He could see nothing because whatever was in progress was being accomplished down inside the barn.

"Firebrands?" asked Sargent, struggling to his feet looking anxious. "Sheriff, what're they doin' down there?"

"Damned if I know, Jim, but I doubt if it'll be firebrands. They couldn't hope to reach the house even on horseback before we'd cut them down. They're not that dumb."

Jim hobbled to a window. The others left the water bucket to also cross over and look out. It was a long, fraught wait. Nothing stirred, there wasn't a sound. Finally though, Tim Holbrook caught the faintest brief glimpse of movement down behind the barn and out the back a short distance. "They're pulling out," he said, scarcely believing that himself. "Watch out the back. I just caught sight of a horse over there."

But for a long time no one else saw anything. The quiet hung and the heat kept building. Sargent had to give it up at last and return to the cot. His leg and hip were causing him considerable anguish. Joe Cane, though, stayed at his window until he finally heard what he was listening for: horsemen quietly riding their animals away at a walk, being very careful to keep the barn always between them and the house full of fighting cattlemen across Sargent's yard.

Joe said what he thought. "They're riding out. They've had enough and are pulling out. Hey, Sheriff, open the door an' let's get a look."

Tim didn't open the door. He heard those tell-tale

sounds too, but was content to just stand there loosening his body for a while. "Let 'em get away first," he said. "Then'll we'll go have a look."

The others also relaxed. Clay Spangler headed for that bottle of rye whisky, uncorked it, tilted back his head and drank. He then held the bottle out to his brother. Ariel also drank. The bottle passed around until Tim Holbrook got it. Finally, he took a couple of good swallows, then opened the bullet-riddled cabin door. Nothing happened. He stepped into the door. Still nothing happened. He turned and jerked his head. All but Jim Sargent trooped outside after him. Jim sank back on his cot with a stifled groan and closed his eyes. Of them all, the fight had taken the most out of him because he'd been injured before it had begun. He was perfectly content to have Holfinger go away. He was equally as content not to see the inside of his bullet-pocked barn, but to let the others look, then perhaps later describe to him how much damage had been done.

CHAPTER FOURTEEN

THE BARN, even more than Sargent's cabin, showed the results of a terrific battle. There were carbine and pistol casings lying everywhere. There was even a streamer of blood across a cribbing pole tied inside a stall. Someone had been nicked. But as Holbrook considered that blood he recalled how the other wounded Texan back in town had got back to Holfinger's cow-camp, and had then joined his friends when they rode away. Evidently this second injured man was hurt no worse than the first one had been.

Joe Cane came back to the front door from out the back where he'd looked from beneath a tipped-down hatbrim seeking Holfinger's crew. He said, "Jim's goin' to explode when he sees the inside of his barn. Between the two bunches of us we must've busted half the siding on the south wall."

Bert Morgan said, "I'll help him put it back up, when the time comes."

Tim Holbrook strolled on out the back to also study the direction of Holfinger's tracks and seek his dust far out. He had no illusions that this repulse had broken the back of Holfinger's angry spirit. He returned to the others and said he had to get back to town. At once they protested.

"At least wait until we hitch Jim's wagon," exclaimed Joe Cane. "Then the lot of us'll head in together."

Tim agreed to that. He and Joe returned to the cabin to carry Jim down to the barn. The others rigged out horses, put them on the pole and made fast their traces. Ariel Spangler put a layer of loose hay upon the floorboards of the outfit then returned to the barn for horses. He and his brother as well as Seldon Stubbs had left their horses a mile southward hidden in a draw. The three of them went after those mounts as soon as Joe Cane and Sheriff Holbrook came slowly forth supporting Sargent between them.

Getting Jim into the wagon wasn't easy, for he saw the inside of his barn and got mad all over again. He insisted that he be allowed to look in there. Joe Cane helped him over there.

"I'll kill 'em," he swore, shaking a big fist with his carbine in it. "I'll salivate every blessed one of 'em for that. Sheriff, you got any idea how hard it is to come by planed timber in this country? That there barn was my pride an' joy. I put danged near all the money I made for two years into it. I'll kill every one of them, by golly, and that's a plumb promise."

"Jim," said Tim Holbrook, when he could finally get a word in. "Jim, it wasn't Holfinger who did that. It was us firing into the barn from your house."

But Sargent would not be placated. "All the same if they hadn't been in there we wouldn't have had to wreck my barn, consarn it. They had no business . . ."

"Get in the wagon, Jim," said Holbrook a trifle sharply. "We're wasting time."

They boosted him over the tailgate. He had to shut up in order to clench his teeth when the pain hit, which was a relief to the others. Cane made him comfortable while Holbrook and Morgan went after their saddle animals. The last man to get settled was Joe Cane. He got his horse, saddled it and led it out to be lashed to the tailgate. The other two were sitting their mounts when Joe finally climbed to the wagon seat, bent to lift the lines, and looked around at the hard rattle of running horses coming in from the south. It was the Spangler brothers and Seldon Stubbs.

The small cavalcade got under way, finally, with Holbrook and Bert Morgan out-riding ahead and the other mounted men flanking the wagon. It was very hot, the air was still and heavy, and a mile onward Jim asked around if anyone had a canteen. Bert Morgan was the only man who had one. He dropped back and gave it to Sargent, then loped on ahead to resume his position beside Tim Holbrook.

Where they struck a fairly level stretch of trail with good visibility all around Bert said, "Sheriff, those big fellers back there, the ones called Spangler, how long've they known I was in the hills?"

"About a week after you arrived here. You made most of your camps on their range. They found several of them while riding and told me someone was skulkin' around. Folks thought at first you were either a rustler or an outlaw on the dodge."

"And you—what'd you think?"

"That you might be an outlaw on the run, Bert, but that you weren't an assassin because after a couple of weeks without you taking a shot at anyone, it didn't seem likely you were here for that purpose. Then Grace recognised you. After that I knew what you were doing here. But tell me; how did you know Brent was coming down here to the Bullhead country?"

"I trailed Brent to Carbon City in Colorado. There, I ran into some fellers in a poker game who knew Brent. They said when he left he mentioned Bullhead, but he also said he had to go first to a little place below Denver and transact some business. I didn't trail him down to Denver, but cut out straight for Bullhead. I wanted to get the lay of the land before he did." Bert gave his head a little doleful wag. "But hell, it turned out to be a pretty big country. Then, too, you know how Brent works. He's as elusive as a grass snake. It took me another two weeks, nearly, to finally locate his camp. That's why I took that shot at him back in the hills when I could've gotten away from Holfinger's crew by just keeping quiet and sneakin' off. I'd waited too long, ridden too far, to let the chance slip away when I finally got him in my sights." Morgan turned towards Holbrook. "But what puzzles me is my sister being here."

"Coincidence," said Holbrook. "She came here about two years back. I never asked why she chose Bullhead, but she did. Anyway, until she showed up here we never had a decent café. She was a big hit right off, Bert. And I can tell you somethin' else; she's been plenty worried about you. You're all the family she's got left."

Bert dropped his head a moment, saying nothing, then raised it to cast a long look out and around. He said no more about his personal affairs. They came to a narrow place where the trail bent around a fat hillside. Holbrook booted his horse out to pass around and see beyond. Bert did the same.

The naked hills were empty. Even the hilltops where Holbrook half expected to see a sentinel watching for them, showed nothing. When Morgan commented on this Holbrook told him it meant nothing; that the customary way for stalkers to operate in the treeless, brush-less Buckskin Hills, was to lie belly-down in tall grass where they could see without being seen.

But if that was the case they neither saw such a sentinel nor were fired upon by one. They got almost to the Stubbs' place through winding hills before Seldon came up front to ask if Tim didn't think they should stop at the ranch for a spell, water their stock and give Sargent a respite from the bumping. Holbrook said no. But he also said he thought Seldon and the Spanglers should veer off and go among the ranches to make certain everyone was safe.

"Who?" Seldon demanded. "My wife, my brother's wife, even our paw, is in Bullhead. There's no women or kids at the Spangler place, the Cane place or Jim

Sargent's ranch—and the only other one would be the Bronson ranch. There's no one left out there either, Sheriff. Everyone's either already in town or ridin' right here with this wagon."

Holbrook thought a moment then agreed with that. He began speculating on what Holfinger would do next. It occurred to him that Holfinger might also figure out that the ranches were unprotected. He did not put it past Holfinger to fire the ranches or turn his Texans loose to plunder them. Such behaviour was not beyond Holfinger. But it stuck in the back of Holbrook's mind that with Brent finally openly operating with Holfinger's riders, the dandified Texan just might decide on cutting down the principal men he considered his enemies. If this were so, then Holfinger would be somewhere on ahead waiting for Tim Holbrook, with Idaho Brent hidden in some good vantage point with his guns and his spyglass.

He decided to take one man and ride on ahead. "Stay with the wagon," he told young Seldon Stubbs. "Morgan and I'll have a look ahead. We're getting near the pass out of the hills. If there's an ambush it's got to be up ahead." He jerked his head at Bert. The pair of them loped ahead. Seldon watched them a moment, then signalled for one of the Spanglers to come up and ride the lead position with him. Jim Sargent's rough profanity could be heard some distance off every time they struck a bad stretch of trail or a wheel dropped into a chuck-hole. Another thing, besides his swollen, purple hip which troubled Jim was the heat. He lay unprotected from it upon his bed of scratchy straw. Altogether, his trip was not at all pleasant.

The hills buckled into stifling canyons and rose up to form great tawny mounds. Now and then, where a vagrant breeze touched the tall, grainy heads of the grass, shadows rippled. The silence was seemingly endless. Little bunches of cattle drifted here and there seeking shade, and several little bands of mares and colts stood on the heights, less mindful of the heat.

Up where Holbrook rode with Bert Morgan the land began to perceptibly tilt eastward, all the little side-canyons running together down in one major debouchment which ended at the onward pass and out upon the prairie beyond the hills. The farther along those two rode the nearer they came to the safety of open country.

"No sign," muttered young Morgan. "Maybe they aren't going to try anything after all, Sheriff."

"Maybe," agreed Tim drily. "All the same it'll pay to keep a sharp watch."

Holbrook came around a little bend and could finally see the onward plain far ahead through the pass. He shook his head. If Holfinger didn't try to ambush them before they got out of the hills, he was missing his last good chance to do so. But if he didn't, then Holfinger had something better in mind. That was the main trouble in dealing with a man like Arnold Holfinger: it was nearly impossible to predict his actions.

"Whoa," murmured Bert, lifting an arm to point up a southward slope. "Watch up there, Sheriff. Maybe it was a shadow or my imagination, but it seemed like a man's head and chest stickin' up out of the grass."

"Keep riding," ordered Holbrook. "Act natural."

They went along another few yards probing that southerly top-out from beneath their lowered hat-brims. A dirty old cloud, fat and high, drifted overhead to cast a moving shadow over the yonder hilltop. For as long as it took to pass, the heights were greyly darkened. Then it passed and Tim saw him too. One solitary man up there low in the grass watching the canyon trail. The sentinel apparently believed himself safe from detection, and under ordinary circumstances he would have been, too. But these were not ordinary circumstances; Holbrook and Bert Morgan had been under attack; they were now expecting another attack. They were keyed to the imminence of danger.

"The question is," muttered Holbrook, "is he alone and keeping watch, or is the rest of his crew up there with him?"

"Damned bad spot down in this arroyo," responded Morgan. "Shooting downhill's no cinch, but if they can stop us in here—bottle us up at both ends—they can make their shots count."

Holbrook reflected on that. Brent the assassin knew how to accomplish such a thing. So did Arnold Holfinger, evidently. But in order to achieve their murderous ends they'd have to split up, part of them riding back around the wagon-party, part of them getting down into the onward pass to seal them off. That wouldn't leave very many men up there on that hilltop.

"I think," said Sheriff Holbrook slowly, "the thing to do is make a run for it and take a chance on the men that're planted on ahead at the end of the pass. You drop back and warn the others. Tell Jim to hang on. Tell Joe to whip up the team. Tell Seldon and the Spanglers to bunch up close behind the wagon. When they hear me shoot, head down towards the pass like their lives depended upon it—because they will."

Bert started to argue. "Hell, Sheriff; there's got to be at least three of 'em on ahead in hiding. You won't stand much of a . . ."

"Do like I told you," snapped Holbrook, turning a cold look on the younger man. "Tomorrow we'll talk about what we *should* have done, or *could* have done. Right now there's no time for that. Go on back."

Morgan slowed his animal, turned and let it start walking back up the trace. He didn't hurry. Tim Holbrook kept his head tilted sufficiently to see that sentinel up there raise a little more out of the grass to watch. He was banking on Morgan's slow gait fooling the watcher into thinking it was just a routine business, Morgan drifting back to see how the wagon was coming along.

The watcher did nothing. At least as far as Tim could see he simply kept watching and gave no kind of a signal. The trail fell away into a shady trough between the hills. Jim Sargent would ordinarily have enjoyed this shade, but he wouldn't now, for by the time the wagon reached it, the rig would be careening and murderously bouncing.

Holbrook slowed his horse slightly so he'd be able to keep that spy up there in view without turning his head. Finally, as he was at the end of his onward route, where he could see the man without obviously looking up at him, the sentinel dropped down and re-emerged a few yards farther along. He was pacing Holbrook. Where he appeared the next time was upon the east slope of his same high roll of grassland. There, Tim saw him hold his carbine barrel so that sunlight struck it. He was giving the signal.

Tim tightened his hand on the reins, reached carefully for his sixgun, drew it and held it in his lap. The ambushers on ahead couldn't be far off now. The hair along the back of his head stiffened. He turned his attention upon every shadow, every side-canyon, every stand of tall grass where the assassins might be lying. He couldn't use his carbine for to draw it out now would be a dead give-away, and he doubted that the killers would be in pistol range. Still, he'd use the .45 to signal with, then he'd turn tail and rush back to lend support to the wagon when it started speeding ahead. There was little else one man could do.

CHAPTER FIFTEEN

BUT A MAN'S best plans often fail simply because they do not coincide with the plans of others. Holbrook was gripping his sixgun and narrowly studying the roundabout slopes and shadows when he came around the last curve before dropping down the final stretch of road to the pass, and there he caught the faint scent of roiled dust. The ambushers had to be close now. He let his mount amble along on a loose rein.

At the pass itself the hills dropped back a little. There were several gulleys down there where men could easily be lying in wait. But what Holbrook was looking for was the place where Holfinger's men had secreted their horses.

He didn't find it, so evidently the ambushers had come down from the heights or had ridden out on the plain first, and had left their animals out there, beyond view of anyone approaching the pass from within the hills.

He turned casually and ran a quick, hard look up

that southward slope for sight of the sentinel up there. The man was nowhere in sight.

That dust scent got stronger. On ahead, on both sides of the trail, were little narrow erosion washes, deep enough to hide men, and gloomy enough in their depths to conceal movement. That, Holbrook decided, had to be where the bushwhackers were waiting. He halted, turned sideways as though totally innocent of suspicion, and listened for the wagon. He heard it coming, but well around the last bend. He let the .45 lie in his lap and started to make a smoke, at the same time studying the onward twin gullies on opposite sides of the trail. When he lit up he caught sight of vague movement on his right, down in the depths of one gulch. He flicked the match, took a deep-down inhalation, picked up his sixgun and held it tightly in the right hand. The wagon's sounds were getting closer. Within moments it would come around the last bend, along with its mounted escort.

He smoked a moment longer, killed the quirley on his saddlehorn, dropped it, raised his sixgun, aimed blindly into the shadowy place where he'd sighted that faint movement, and fired. The thunderous crash of that gunshot down in the canyon sounded like the blast of a cannon. His horse gave a violent jump and landed swapping ends. Holbrook hooked the beast hard, ran back towards the bend where the wagon was appearing, saw Bert and Ariel Spangler out ahead, and shouted to them at the same moment several carbines opened up from down where the sheriff had shot into that little gully.

Joe Cane bawled at the top of his lungs. His team hit their collars in panic and over the wild lunging of the wagon arose the astonished, pained howl of Jim

Sargent in the back, hanging on for dear life and furiously cursing.

Seldon and big Ariel Spangler jumped their horses out as Holbrook whirled and started straight back down the trail. Up ahead men suddenly sprang up, firing. There were four of them. Sheriff Holbrook's horse was stung across the rump and bolted with the bit in his teeth carrying his rider straight down where those gunmen were trying to catch him in their sights. Within seconds he was within sixgun range. He rode low and half twisted in the saddle. A bullet carried away his hat and another one came so close he felt its lethal breath.

Farther back, riding straight up and firing, came Seldon and Ariel Spangler. Farther back Bert Morgan and Clay Spangler were also firing, using carbines. The fight was savage for as long as it lasted, but because the horses were running in terror they carried the men right down towards the ambushers in flashing moments and none of the participants could ever afterwards entirely agree on anything except that it was the wildest of rides.

Holbrook caught one glimpse of Arnold Holfinger down in that draw with three of his men. He snapped two shots at him and after the second one Holfinger jumped aside with a cry and tried to get out of sight in the shadows. One of his Texans stood wide-legged, levering and firing. The other one shot from down on one knee. The standing man suddenly threw up both arms and staggered backwards. Holbrook fired point-blank at him and the rangerider fell, striking his kneeling companion.

Holbrook swept past, his horse still stampeding with the bit in its teeth. Behind him came young Stubbs and big Ariel Spangler. They raked the arroyo with gunfire, shooting carbines one-handed. Farther back, as they came into closer range, the other Spangler and young Bert Morgan also poured in more bullets. Even Joe Cane, barely able to keep his seat upon the drunkenly careening wagon, was holding his useless lines in one hand, firing his sixgun with the other hand. Bawling at the top of his outraged voice was Jim Sargent, clutching sideboards with both hands.

Holbrook couldn't regain control of his mount until he was out of the pass and a half mile across the yonder plain, but eventually he got the horse turned in a big circle and headed back, at the same time he got the animal slowed sufficiently to manage him with the reins.

The wagon horses hit the pass in a dead run. Fortunately the onward land was smooth and flat. Seldon and Bert Morgan were racing in low on each side, to try for a hold of the team's bridles. They got the wagon slowed by the time Tim Holbrook came up on his heaving animal, and between the three of them they got the team halted. The last ones out of the pass were the Spangler brothers, both riding straight up as though scorning to drop low over their horse's shoulders, and firing backwards from twisted positions in their saddles.

Joe Cane had shot his sixgun empty. So had Tim Holbrook. They started reloading as soon as they saw the Spanglers break clear and hit the prairie. Jim Sargent was calling on someone to help him out of the blasted wagon.

"I'll die right here," he raged, "before I'll ride another foot behind Joe and those damned runaway horses!"

Back in the pass there was dust and gunsmoke, but no sign of their ambushers. Holbrook motioned for Joe Cane to ease out and keep driving. "You're still in rifle range," he said. "Move on a little farther then stop."

Joe flicked the lines. The horses lunged, knocking Jim Sargent's head against the springs under the front seat. He swore and dropped down, grasping the sideboards again. But the team had run itself out. Joe tooled the wagon along handily. Farther back the Spanglers loped up, halted, and wordlessly turned to reloading. One of them finished first and said, glancing over his shoulder, "Those damned fools; only four of 'em an' they had the guts to think they could stop us."

Tim put up his reloaded sixgun and hauled out his carbine. "It's not over yet," he said. "Look yonder."

Up the trail four horsemen were whipping their horses straight down from the direction the wagon had just taken, using the flat of their carbines to get the last ounce of speed from their mounts. Up the southward hill another horseman was coming down towards the roadway, and off to the left three men were running up out of a little gloomy gully on foot, gesticulating and howling for the mounted men to hurry.

Gunshots sounded flat where the Texans prematurely opened fire, still inside the pass. That rider up the southward hillside suddenly slid his horse rapidly down almost to the level land, sprang off, dropped flat and raised his rifle. Holbrook, watching that one, had a premonition. He turned and frantically waved at Joe Cane, who immediately looked over his shoulder instead of whipping up his team to a faster gait. The rifleman up there fired, his weapon making a whip-

E

lash of flat sound. Of all Holfinger's men, this one showed the most coolness, the least excitement. That had been Tim Holbrook's premonition: that was Idaho Brent up there.

One of the wagon horses gave a great lunge ahead, then dropped, shot through the head from a distance of at least two hundred yards. Joe bowled out a mighty curse, not at once willing to believe any of Holfinger's men could shoot like that. Holbrook sprang down and rushed over to cut the dead horse loose of the wagon, but even as he frantically slashed harness leather he knew Brent had stopped them cold out there.

One of the Spanglers was riding a combination horse —saddle and harness—he dismounted without a word, ignoring the oncoming howling Texans and their wild gunfire, began off-saddling to lead his horse over and put it in beside the surviving team animal, but he never completed his work. A bullet came out of nowhere and big Ariel, the eldest of the Spangler brothers, crumpled without a sound. Holfinger's mounted men were converging upon the hamstrung men around their wagons.

"Cut 'em both loose," Holbrook shouted as Joe Cane leapt down to help. "Up-end the wagon!"

Up his sidehill Idaho Brent was slowly drawing another bead. In the canyon Arnold Holfinger and his two surviving cowboys ran breathlessly out through the pass onto the plain and yelled at the mounted riders who had preceded them to make a run on the halted men, clustering around the wagon to tip it over for their fortification.

Joe Cane's saddlehorse, lashed to the tailgate, set back, broke loose, and went racing away. The remaining team animal did the same, harness-tugs whipping around his hind legs scurling up streamers of dust.

Bert Morgan grabbed Jim Sargent out of the wagon just before the others turned the wagon over. Jim was bawling for his guns all the time he was being hauled clear.

Holfinger's attacking riders made their first wild rush. They caught a withering fire from the dismounted men around the wagon and checked themselves, veering off. Up his hill, Idaho Brent seemed content to engage in a long-range duel. He would fire, study the effect, lever up and settle low to fire again. Finally, Holfinger and his two surviving dismounted Texans dropped down and fired from kneeling positions. They, and Idaho Brent, were the only attackers whose accuracy was adequate.

Lead hit the wagon and went no further; the bottom slats were old dried oak, as hard as iron. While Bert and Seldon rolled Jim Sargent over into the safety of that oaken protection, Tim Holbrook and Clay Spangler went after Ariel. He had a deep groove alongside his upper head which had nearly peeled away a strip of scalp four inches long. The wound bled profusely. When they got his great bulk back behind the wagon, Clay put aside his carbine and made a rough bandage of his brother's neckerchief. He wrapped this cloth tightly around Ariel's head and staunched a good deal of the bleeding. When Clay turned to pick up his carbine again, Jim Sargent was bending over the thing from a prone position, using the up-ended wagon-box as his rest, and was trading long-range shots with Idaho Brent, up the far southward slope.

Holfinger's four riders trotted back where Arnold was kneeling and firing with two others. They dismounted and Holfinger stood up to converse with them. This removed five guns from the fight, and a lessening of the battle ensued. It gave Tim Holbrook a chance to survey the damage and their chances.

The damage was considerable. Without the team they could not hope to move Jim Sargent any further. They had one man unconscious—Ariel Spangler—and another man—Jim Sargent—unable to stand up. Their numbers had been whittled down, but so had the odds against them. One of Holfinger's Texans was dead back up the canyon where the ambush had taken place. Idaho Brent, however, was still uninjured. So were the balance of Holfinger's crew. To top that off, the Texans had mobility. They could ride around behind the wagon, which Tim was certain Holfinger would order them to do before he broke up that little conference he was having up near the foot of the pass.

Bullhead was tantalisingly close, and yet it was also discouragingly distant. No one in town could hear the battle nor see the dust and gunsmoke, and yet if the defenders dared catch their horses and spring into the saddle, they could reach town in something like a half hour of hard riding or a full hour of slow riding.

Holfinger's parley broke up. His mounted men got back astride, turned and started walking their horses far to the left, out and around, so as to approach the wagon's defenders from the rear, exactly as Holbrook had anticipated. He told the others what they could now expect—attack from behind and from in front simultaneously, with Idaho Brent trying hard to bring them down one at a time from up his sidehill.

Jim Sargent, still in pain but at least no longer suffering from the buffeting he'd received in the wild ride down out of the hills, turned and croaked a tough observation. "Our weapons shoot just as far as theirs. Sheriff, an' if they stand still for accuracy, we'll have stationary targets too. As I see it, we at least got this damned wagon in front of us, an' they got nothin'."

"They got Brent," exclaimed young Bert Morgan, peering up the hill where Holfinger's hired assassin still lay, occasionally firing. "Right this minute I'd trade all I own for one long-barrelled rifle."

The Texans continued to circle around through the heat and glare of afternoon, neither hastening nor firing. When they got half behind the forted men they were in the way of Idaho Brent; if he fired and missed striking something solid near the wagon, his bullet might carry out far enough, although spent, to injure a rider. Brent raised up and made a slow gesture for the horsemen to get out of his way, but they ignored it and kept on with their circling ride. Bert Morgan tried a long, uphill shot the moment Brent exposed himself. The bullet must have come very close because Brent suddenly dropped back down and scooped up his own carbine to shoot back angrily. His slug scuffed dirt ten feet in front of the wagon.

There was a little artificial shade behind the wagon-box; it didn't particularly cool the defenders at all, but it aided their sightings because they did not have any glare in their eyes. Bert Morgan tried another of those looping high shots. It surprised them all when Brent suddenly moved back, and thus got out of range.

"Good shootin'," said Clay Spangler to Bert Morgan. "You may get him yet."

CHAPTER SIXTEEN

THE MOUNTED Texans halted just beyond carbine range and dismounted. One man stayed back with their horses. The other three started inching forward, at the same time fanning out so the defenders could not get in any lucky shots.

They did not fire, which interested Tim Holbrook until Bert Morgan called his attention to a new manoeuvre up ahead where Holfinger was beckoning Idaho Brent down where Holfinger and his two companions stood idly waiting.

"Something new," Morgan grunted, peering from eyes pinched nearly closed. "Holfinger's going to use Brent to spot-shoot at us, and I'd bet he's goin' to use all the others to distract us from shootin' back."

"Might be," conceded Holbrook, watching Brent mount his horse, turn northward and start picking his way around the sidehill in Holfinger's direction. "Might be, Bert. You keep close watch. If anything happens call me." Holbrook went over where Clay was working over his unconscious brother. "How's it look?" he asked.

Clay was non-committal as he dampened the drying bandage from Morgan's canteen and rearranged it. "The bleeding's stopped, Sheriff, but it was a pretty hard knock for a man to take alongside the skull." Clay rocked back on his heels to examine his brother's sweaty, grey face. "I just don't know. He'll probably make it all right. But I just don't know."

Tim raised up to look rearward. Those three Texans back there had halted. Seldon Stubbs, concentrating upon those three, said, "They got it figured to a T, Sheriff. They're right now on the very edge of accurate carbine range for us an' for them."

Tim went over to Jim Crawford and Joe Cane, lying side by side and keeping their eyes forward, up where Idaho Brent was finally crossing the last broken country to get up where Arnold Holfinger was awaiting. "Like that young feller said a while back, Sheriff," growled Joe. "I'd give an awful lot right now for a long-barrelled rifle."

Jim Sargent was relaxing, his head lying in the bend of one arm, his shaded eyes fixed dead ahead. When Tim asked how he was making out, Sargent rolled his eyes around and said, "This is pure bliss, bullets an' all, after that consarned ride down out of the hills, Sheriff. Pure bliss."

Tim faintly grinned. "How's the hip, Jim?"

"Twice its normal size and turnin' black, but otherwise there's not much hurt to it. 'Course all I can compare the pain to, for bein' sure it still hurts, is that damned ride Joe gave me."

Evidently Jim had been complaining along the same line before Holbrook came up, because Joe Cane resignedly turned his head in a long-suffering way and regarded Sargent balefully.

"Maybe you'd rather I'd left you up there for Holfinger to fill full of lead," he growled.

Sargent met that irritated glance. "Joe, I never noticed it before, but you're the poorest excuse for a wagon driver I ever saw."

Joe looked at Holbrook. The sheriff looked straight back. He grinned, shrugged, and moved on towards the end of the up-turned wagon. Seldon sang out.

"The ones in back are gettin' some kind of a signal from Holfinger. Look out; we're goin' to get it directly now."

Young Stubbs was correct. Holfinger was waving his hat at arm's length from side to side above his head, a perfect signal to the men far out eastward. They raised their carbines and fired a volley. One slug struck high, the other two fell low, and the fourth one hit the up-raised wagon-tongue.

"Never mind them," called Holbrook. "Keep down and watch out front."

That proved excellent advice, for as soon as the east-ward attackers resumed firing, Arnold Holfinger, Idaho Brent, and the balance of the Texans spread wide and began a slow and careful advance.

Bert Morgan ignored everyone and everything ex-cept Idaho Brent. He fired once to let Brent know he was under personal attack. As before, when Brent had been up the sidehill, young Morgan's slug came close enough to halt Brent and drop him to one knee so he'd make less of a target.

Seldon and Clay Spangler were firing at Holfinger himself. Their shots both fell far short. Holfinger evidently did not realise he was under personal attack and kept advancing. The men behind the wagon far out began a very cautious advance. They were finally within range. Jim Sargent twisted around, rested his carbine upon a wheel-spoke, took long, careful aim and fired. One of the Texans sprang up and went staggering away in a shambling run. Sargent levered up another bullet, aimed, held his breath a second, and squeezed the trigger. That staggering man pitched headlong and did not move again.

That kind of unnerving accuracy shook up the remaining men out there. They dropped flat down and fired rapidly and aimlessly, but all this accomplished was to turn Clay Spangler around to join Jim Sargent in this long-range deadly duel.

Tim knelt near Bert Morgan looking around the edge of the up-turned wagon. He did not fire. The range ahead was still too great for any kind of predictable accuracy, and Tim Holbrook had little faith in luck at this kind of shooting.

He knelt, watching and patiently waiting, until one Texan got too close, then he raised his gun, took a long rest, and kicked up dust less than a foot in front of his target. The Texan dropped and rolled frantically. Holfinger shouted something at the man but there was no response, the Texan had just survived a close brush with death and it had understandably temporarily unnerved him.

The fight suddenly ended with the men eastward going back as far as their dead companion, there to stand up talking and glaring towards the forted-up men at the wagon-box. Out front, the same thing occurred. Arnold Holfinger zigzagged his men over to him. They all walked back through the heat, out of range. There, they fell into gesticulating conversation. Only Idaho Brent remained prone and indifferent to what his companions were doing. He'd discerned that he was being attacked by one defender, and chose to remain out there trading shots with him. The other men behind the wagon would have joined in that fight except that Tim Holbrook, passing among them to check for wounds, quietly asked them not to. Brent belonged to young Bert Morgan, he said, and if they

E*

survived this mess, some day he'd explain all about that to them.

They had only that one canteen. They left it for Clay to use in abating the fever in Ariel's wound, and to alleviate thirst sucked on little pebbles. During each lull they also had time for a smoke. Their shade was getting stronger; was actually beginning to feel cool behind the wagon-box. Seldon said he thought it had to be about four in the afternoon. The others accepted that without comment but time really had very little importance right then.

"What'll that cussed Holfinger think of next?" Clay inquired of Holbrook.

"Darkness," the lawman surmised. "This kind of fighting is a Mexican stand-off with him out in the sun and us holed up behind the wagon. He needs something to off-set our little advantage. I think he'll call it off until it gets dark enough for them to try sneakin' up on us."

"All right," Seldon said, accepting this verbatim. "And what'll we do, Sheriff?"

Tim squinted out where Brent was finally giving up in disgust and going back where the balance of Holfinger's men were, and said, "We'll wait for darkness too, boys. Then, with a little luck, we'll get away from the wagon and let them have it."

The others nodded over this without speaking. They waited for Holbrook to stop watching their enemies and say the rest of it. They lit up and sat slumped in good shade.

"Then," went on the lawman, looking down among them, "we'll try turning the tables, and cut Holfinger's drygulchers to pieces while they're gatherin' around the wagon."

Seldon Stubbs broadly smiled. He liked that plan. So did Joe Cane, although Jim Sargent asked a question which showed that although he wasn't averse to Holbrook's scheme, he had personal doubts about his part in it. "How the hell do I sneak away from here, Sheriff, with one leg useless and the other one not much better?"

Tim turned and pointed where the dead horse lay in his tangled harness. "There's your answer, Jim. We'll rig up a sling and carry you with us."

Joe Cane made a sly grin and winked at the others as he said, "Jim, you'll look right natural, hooked up in that set of work harness."

Sargent grinned back. Tim Holbrook, watching those two hard-faced, rough men, pondered on what it took with some men to bring out humour. He'd known those two a number of years and in all that time had never before seen either of them act as though they knew how to smile or laugh, yet here, with death surrounding them and darkness coming, they found something to be amused about.

He raised up to look both ways. Those eastward Texans had returned to their horses, were astride now and were poking along making that identical huge half-circle around the defenders to arrive back up where Holfinger was standing with the rest of his crew. They rode as men do who have lost spirit; slumped and lethargically indifferent. The last horse had a limp carcass draped across the saddle.

Up near the pass the other attackers were acting restless. Tim could understand that; for one thing they had no cover from the shimmering heat. For another they had no water. And finally, what they'd evidently in full confidence expected to be a hot little triumphant battle with the hill stockmen and the lone cow-county sheriff, had turned out to be quite something else altogether.

Tim's attention was diverted when Ariel Spangler groaned and weakly waved his arms. Clay was beside him changing the bandage when Ariel came around. His heavy features slowly brightened with powerful hope and relief. He said, "Ariel, lie still. You got clipped alongside the head."

Ariel opened his eyes in the shade and blinked around into the watching faces. He started to speak, licked his lips, swallowed and tried again. "What the —hell—did they hit me with, an anvil?"

The men smiled through sweat and dirt and the grime of their long days' battle. Even Bert Morgan came over. His personal duel was temporarily ended; Idaho Brent was no longer in range. He made a cigarette and stuck it between Ariel's ashen lips, lit a match and held it. Spangler took a deep drag and faintly smiled.

"Damned hot out here," he said around the smoke. "And if you think gettin' hung over from too much likker produces a headache, try a bullet grazin' your skull sometime. Sheriff . . .?"

Tim moved in where the prone man could see him better. "Rest easy, Ariel," he said. "You're all right. After nightfall we'll get help."

Ariel removed the cigarette and put a sceptical glance upwards. "After nightfall will we still be needin' it?" he inquired.

Holbrook nodded downward. "Don't worry about them cleanin' us out. They've been tryin' all day and haven't found a way yet. I doubt if they'll have much better luck after dark."

"How'll you move me, Sheriff?"

Clay leaned over his brother and said, "Don't worry about that. If I have to pack you on my back we'll get you clear."

Ariel subsided, lowered the hand holding his smoke and let his eyes drop closed. He drew in a big breath and noisily let it out. The others moved back behind the wagon again to sit in their shade. The long afternoon pulsed on. Now and then someone would peer around where Holfinger's men were, and drop back again with a shrug or a little head-wag. The attackers had sent two of their horsemen back up through the pass, evidently after water, and the balance of them were keeping the vigil, two holding the reins to their mounts in case any of the men behind the wagon should try slipping away towards Bullhead.

It was the proximity of succour that annoyed them. For a while they kept a look outward, believing someone would come along from the direction of town, but no one ever did.

"Too hot," Clay Spangler thought. "Or else there's no cause for folks to be riding out."

"There's cause enough," growled Jim Sargent, "only no one but us and *them* know about it."

Joe Cane was sceptical. "If anyone came along it'd likely be only a solitary rider. The chances of us bein' found by a big crew is pretty unlikely."

Ariel called his brother to him. Those two conversed for a long time apart from the others. Bert Morgan went to Holbrook with an offer to start out right now, and head for town and help. Holbrook declined with a shrewd look.

"We're not so bad off," he said. "Think it over, Bert. We've injured a couple of Holfinger's men and have probably salted down another two. Our only casualty so far is Ariel, and he won't die—at least not yet. All this talk of wantin' help is so much wind in the treetops. Go on back and get in the shade."

Bert did not move off. He said, "Sheriff, I'm kind of anxious to get to Bullhead."

"You'd better get over it," said Tim. "Stick your head up at the wrong time out here and you just might wind up being our first total casualty. Bullhead will keep. So will Grace. Right now we've got Idaho Brent and some others out there."

Young Morgan's gaze turned cynical. "I didn't mean I was *that* anxious to get to Bullhead," he said. "What I meant was, I want to hunt Brent up, kill him, then ride on into Bullhead." He gave his head a little shake. "Nothing's goin' to come between me'n Idaho Brent, Sheriff. Nothing. I've been too long waiting for this time to get here."

Tim felt for his tobacco sack. The afternoon was beginning to swiftly fail. He made a smoke, looked around and back again, offered Bert the makings and put them up after he got a negative headshake. "I know you've been waitin'," he said, lighting up. "And I reckon you're confident of the outcome. But Bert, unless you've also done a heap of practisin', you're going to get killed. I've never seen Brent in action but I've heard enough, and I know enough about his kind. He's not only unprincipled in how he kills, but he's also fast and damned deadly with his gun."

CHAPTER SEVENTEEN

THE SHADOWS thickened steadily once the afternoon began to definitely fade. The defenders behind their wagon rolled over and looked out. Holfinger's men now seemed anxious to get on with it, particularly Idaho Brent who stayed slightly aloof from Holfinger's rangeriders. He'd spent the lull rubbing his rifle and honing the front sight to a clean, coppery finish. He had his horse nearby and squatted in its shade occasionally gazing down where that up-ended ranch wagon stood.

Bert Morgan concentrated on the killer. He watched every move. Sargent, Cane, all the others behind the wagon, also watched Brent, but they were equally as interested in Arnold Holfinger, Jack Sartain, and the other Texans.

Tim Holbrook divided his time between assessing the lengthening gloom, and keeping a close watch ahead for some kind of movement among the attackers. That movement finally came. Holfinger's riders got up, dusted themselves off and started away, breaking up into separate attacking wings, one to the south, one to the north. It was by then getting gloomy enough to mask most of the details of those men, but not their obvious intention of getting the defenders flanked and between two fires.

Jim Sargent watched a moment then bitterly said, "Too bad we can't just burrow in the ground an' let 'em shoot each other over us."

Bert Morgan raised his carbine and tracked Idaho Brent with it as the assassin left his mount and started around to the left, or southward. With nothing more than a hunch to go on, the defenders thought they knew why Brent had gone with that particular segment of the attackers: because he knew that was the direction which would bring him into contact with the man behind the wagon who had consistently tried to make a personal duel out of this battle. Bert had always kept his vigil from the lower end of the up-turned wagon exactly as he was now doing.

Ariel Spangler was sitting up with a carbine across his lap. Powerful recuperative powers had helped him greatly during the long, hot afternoon. He was fretful from thirst but told Tim the headache had subsided considerably. His brother stood beside him looking over the wagon-box where the northerly band of attackers was stealthily passing through hushed dusk.

Seldon Stubbs twisted as Tim Holbrook came over and leaned on the wagon at his side. "How long do we wait?" Seldon asked.

"Until we're sure they can't make out what we're up to."

"That may be too late," stated young Stubbs, watching the southward Texans out where they kept pace with the failing light in their steady advance.

"I don't think so," said Holbrook, and also turned to watch. "I wish I was sure which bunch Holfinger's with."

There was no way to determine that now. It was too murky, and where the Buckskin Hills backgrounded everything, the dusk was settling fastest, making identification impossible except in a very general way.

It was that particular darkness Tim kept watching.

Those backgrounding hills helped Holfinger's men enormously. They cut off the sun and spread sooty shadows long before the last rays touched the wagon-box.

"Damned hills," muttered Seldon.

Holbrook had no comment. He meant to use that same advantage, but he'd have to cut it fine because of the delay in those spokes of darkness reaching down to his barricade. It eventually happened though; there was a scarlet stain lying outward one moment, then the sun sank, the gloom swept in, and Holbrook, no longer able to make out their furtive attackers, moved swiftly.

"Clay, you and Bert get your brother between you. Joe, you and Seldon get Jim on his feet. We're moving out. Fast now. They'll be closing in from both sides in the dark."

"Where?" asked Joe Cane, bending to give Sargent a hand upwards.

"Follow me," said Holbrook, and stepped around the wagon, northward. The others looked momentarily startled. All afternoon this had been the one direction they'd dared not even expose themselves. Then Joe Cane grinned.

"Be damned," he muttered. "That's right; they'll be expectin' us to fall back towards town. They won't be expectin' us to head northward. Come on, Jim; lean on me'n Seldon."

He led them soundlessly forward, battered and parched and filthy from sweat, gunsmoke, and prairie dust, cautioning them to be very careful, to not make a sound. They had to stop once when Ariel got dizzy, but it was only a brief halt, then they went on ahead, always straight northward.

Tim Holbrook had in mind getting control of those horses up near the entrance to the pass. Their own animals had long since departed. With the horses, and the moonless night, they could possibly turn the tables and put Holfinger on the defensive. They had to get those horses and they had to get close enough to the pass to reach some kind of shelter, in case Holfinger eventually discovered where they'd gone, and Tim had no doubts about that not happening at all. Holfinger wouldn't be fooled for long. Neither would his hired killer.

Somewhere rearward someone fired a gun. At once Tim hissed for them to halt while he walked back a short distance to listen. It was by then too dark to see anything farther than a hundred feet in any direction. The stars were out but their light was weak and watery. There were no more gunshots. Someone had evidently been nervous enough to shoot at a shadow or perhaps at one of the opposite advancing men. Tim returned and flagged the others onward again. He took them far enough forward to be safe from inadvertent discovery, although they were still within carbine-range when he finally halted and whispered for Jim and Ariel to be eased down upon the ground.

Bert Morgan came forward and volunteered to slip back to see what the Texans were doing. Tim shook his head; they'd find out soon enough what Holfinger was up to, now that he'd discovered his enemies had escaped him.

It was Jim Sargent, low enough to see it, who called their attention to a little flare of light down by the wagon. "Tryin' to read the sign," Jim opined. "Tryin' to figure from our tracks which way we went." He snorted. "Damned fools. If they didn't see us north or south, then we only could've gone two ways."

Tim agreed with this, but he thought it through still further. Holfinger and Brent, especially the latter, he thought, would soon enough determine which direction to take in stalking the defenders. They'd send a couple of men trotting southward and a couple trotting northward. The most likely signal would be a pistol shot.

Tim was correct. Young Stubbs picked up the sound of a man coming towards them from his prone position with one ear pushed against the ground. He sat up, hissed to draw their attention, and pointed westward with a rigid arm.

Rawboned, tough, Joe Cane stepped up beside Tim Holbrook and jerked his head. Tim agreed. He motioned for the others to sit perfectly still, then started off with Joe.

They walked carefully ahead, carbines up and ready, the distance between them something like a hundred feet; just far enough so that each could dimly make out the other, but not so close they might stumble onto Holfinger's scout together.

Tim got down to listen, once, and made out the faint reverberations of the oncoming man. He was veering over towards Joe Cane. Tim altered course to intercept him, but he didn't turn sharply enough. He was still a considerable distance off when he suddenly heard someone make a furious grunt. After that there was the sound of furious struggle and threshing where two men had met in fierce combat. He sprang ahead, making directly for that sound. When he saw them he could surmise what had happened. Cane had also picked up the sound of his approaching enemy; had dropped flat and when the Texan came up, had sprang at him giving the Texan no time to draw and fire his warning shot.

It was Jack Sartain, toughest of the Texans. He was nearly Joe's size and every bit as powerful. Joe had Sartain's right wrist locked in a vice-like hold preventing the Texan from drawing his gun. The second Joe saw Tim emerge from the night he panted, "Get his gun!" Holbrook tried and Sartain lashed at him with a booted foot. Tim bent, caught the Texan's belt, heaved, then wrenched away the .45 as Sartain tried to break clear. Joe suddenly released Sartain's wrist and aimed a short, vicious blow to his jaw. Sartain dropped his head and the fist grazed upwards knocking off the Texan's hat. Cane arched his body, flung Sartain aside and whipped up to his feet. Sartain rolled away from Holbrook, who was balancing the Texan's pistol to get a chance to hit Sartain over the head with it, and also sprang upright. He began circling to the right, watching Joe Cane, and Joe turned with him, but always kept his feet together, his legs bent at the knees to jump.

Holbrook could have shot Sartain but that would have given Holfinger the signal as much as though Sartain had fired the shot himself. Cane seemed to read Tim's mind, for he growled, "Stay out of it. I've always wanted a chance at this one."

Tim stepped back and watched. He knew how Sartain fought—in powerful, destructive lunges. He said, "Keep your right cocked, Joe. He'll rush you."

Sartain did rush, but before Joe had his right fist cocked. He caught Cane with a savage attack of lefts and rights. Joe gasped from a hard strike in the middle and turned to one side to absorb the rest of that punishment until he could catch his breath. Sartain fought like a man venting all his frustrations and hatreds. He rocked Cane with a left, then belted him high with a grazing right. He tore into Joe without a let-up, and Cane finally gave ground, turning numb along one side. He backed off to get away. Sartain kept after him. Joe took a big sidewards step and finally got clear. But he had to keep side-stepping to throw Sartain off balance, and finally, the last time Sartain rushed him, Joe sprang back the opposite way letting the dark Texan flail air. Then Joe moved in from off to one side and behind. He caught Sartain under the ear, wilting him, he belted him under the ribs and walked in flat-footed with his right cocked, finally, so that when Sartain came heavily around, Joe caught him flush in the mouth. Claret spewed, Sartain's head whipped back and his knees buckled. He dropped both arms and fell like stone.

Joe dropped beside the Texan without a word and began yanking off his trouser belt and his shell-belt. He was still white-hot with rage. He lashed the Texan's ankles, then roughly turned him over and lashed his wrists behind his back. Not until he was getting up-right again did he speak.

"I ought to kill him," he told Holbrook. "I ought to put the boots to him." Then Cane held up his left hand for Tim to examine. "Broke," he snarled. "Broke the knuckles on his damned skull."

Tim shoved Sartain's .45 into his waistband and reached over. Joe flinched and quietly swore. The hand was broken, there was no question about that. Tim was turning away when a man suddenly appeared through the westerly night, saw them standing over Jack Sartain, and gasped as he went for his gun. Tim spun and dropped at the same he streaked for his hip-holster. None of them had time for any second thoughts. Tim fired a fraction of a second ahead of the Texan, whose bullet ploughed up dirt in front of Joe Cane, who was also drawing.

At once, down the westward night, men called to one another. They were advancing eastward towards the pass, which meant that Holfinger already had discerned which direction his enemies had taken. Tim rolled clear as the Texan fell beside him, shot twice, once by Holbrook, once by Joe Cane. As Tim jumped up a gun lanced the night from the west. He turned with Joe and ran back towards the others. They had to call out to avoid being shot by mistake by their friends, and those calls pinpointed their actual position for Holfinger's attackers. At once probing shots came out of the dark night where Holfinger's riders were fanned out as they advanced.

Bert, Jim, the Spanglers, returned that fire when Joe and Tim Holbrook got back to them. There was no time for explanations. Tim said: "Spread out; be damned careful. They're coming straight at us. If we get separated he damned careful who you shoot at." He looked for Bert Morgan with the intention of keeping Bert with him. But Bert had already faded out in the darkness. He and Joe closed ranks to give Clay a chance to help his injured brother get away, and to also give young Seldon Stubbs time to get Jim Sargent to his feet.

Holfinger's ringing shout rose over the gunfire. "Remember what I said! One thousand for each one you kill an' *two* thousand for that damned lawman!"

Tim fired towards that voice, and immediately four guns shot back, aiming at the muzzleblast of Holbrook's gun. One bullet cut through his trouser leg near the hip and seared the flesh. Holbrook felt the stickiness of blood running down inside his trousers but the wound stung rather than hurt. It did not impede his swift withdrawal either, retreating backwards with the others.

Cane yelled something and sprang away after doing that. The minute a gun flashed towards the sound of Joe's shout, he fired his sixgun three times so fast it sounded almost like one rolling gunshot. A man screamed down in the westerly night. Joe's ruse had worked perfectly.

Tim was alone. Behind him were the others of his party. Off to his right somewhere was Joe Cane with his broken left hand and his good right hand. Joe tried that yelling trick again but that time when the Texan's fired towards the sound they too sprang clear. Joe fired and hit nothing, then he had to run backwards and let the Spanglers take his place at the firing until he could reload.

Tim retreated too, his leg turning numb but with its stickiness spreading all the way downward into his boot. Holfinger's men suddenly ceased firing. Tim stopped to listen. He heard men moving out there but could not determine what they were up to, so he fell all the way back where the others were also tensely listening. The only one of them not present was young Bert Morgan. Tim swore in a furious whisper about that. This was no time for young Bert to try getting in among their enemies; he could be killed accidentally by his own friends doing that.

CHAPTER EIGHTEEN

IT TOOK several minutes for the men around Tim Holbrook to understand why the battling Texans had broken off the fight. Clearly, being farther westward, Holfinger's men could hear sounds approaching from that direction better than Tim's crew could. But they eventually also heard them.

"Riders," breathed Joe Cane, sounding as though he did not believe it himself. "Horsemen coming from the direction of town, by gawd!"

"With a wagon," said someone. Tim didn't get a chance to determine who that second speaking man was. Holfinger's shout rang out loud and clear.

"Get to the horses!"

The horses Holfinger's men had left were behind Holbrook's companions over by the mouth of the pass. Tim had barely time enough to cry a warning when Holfinger's men made a hard rush forward, blazing away to cut a path through in their desperation. Joe Cane went down, rolled over with a roar of indignation and got back up as far as one knee, shot through one leg. He fired straight at the oncoming Texans not bothering to roll after each shot. The Spanglers, still using carbines, levered and fired as methodically as though they were at a turkey shoot; they were heavy, phlegmatic men anyway.

Seldon and Jim Sargent lay side by side blazing away. Tim Holbrook dropped flat and tracked the onrushing men by their gunblasts. Far out, behind the Texans, a number of sharp cries of alarm sounded. Evidently the riders approaching from the direction of Bullhead were moving in directly behind the Texans and had bullets slicing the night around them. They broke ranks in an audible rush, breaking away to the left and the right.

A triumphant scream rose up over the tumult of battle that made Tim Holbrook pause to look southward. He knew that voice and it took only a second to realise the purpose behind that yell. Bert Morgan had found his enemy. There was a violent exchange of gunshots down in that southerly direction, then silence. Tim froze, staring in that direction. Then the same voice cried out again in the same way, and Tim turned back to his own work. Bert had evened an old, old score, and had survived.

Clay Spangler's rifle was shot out of his hands. He looked stunned and was a moment recovering sufficiently to reach down for his holstered sixgun. Ariel was sitting up and firing from the hip with his Winchester, his bandaged head dark red in the night, blending with the shadows. The smell of burnt powder was strong enough to burn the eyes. Tim saw someone trying to fight his way around to the north, and rolled in that direction. There was no time to think, to plan more than the simplest, instinctive manoeuvre. He had no idea who that Texan was trying to slip around and reach the horses, he only knew he wanted to stop him from getting away.

Then, as they came closer, he saw the grey front of a ruffled shirt and the long length of a Prince Albert coat. *Arnold Holfinger!*

The Texan fired once at the blaze of Tim's gun, realising one of the defenders was trying to intercept him. He ran back a little way and fired again. Neither of those bullets was even close. Tim rolled further, turning his back on the raging battle, propped his pistol in the cupped fist of his free hand and waited for another glimpse of that pale shirtfront. When Holfinger turned to fire, Tim squeezed the trigger. Arnold shot, but the bullet went high overhead, then he fell, rolled half over and threw up his pistol again. Tim cocked his own weapon and squeezed once more. The hammer dropped with a little 'click' of sound upon an empty casing. He was shot out. He could see Holfinger's gun plainly. It was aimed straight at him. From that distance it would be hard for Holfinger to miss. But as Arnold's thumb reached for the hammer, the barrel began to tilt. It drooped more and more, its solid weight dragging Holfinger's hand and wrist downward. Tim stared from a distance of less than a hundred feet, barely breathing until the sixgun slid out of Holfinger's fingers and fell to the ground.

Tim heard men shouting behind him but scarcely heeded them. He didn't even hear the gunfire begin to diminish as the beaten, leaderless Texans, caught at last between the stubborn gunfire of Tim's men in front, and the fresh guns of the townsmen from behind, yelled out they were quit, that they'd had enough.

He got up slowly, very cautiously, and started ahead where Holfinger lay half on his side, half on his stomach, his hatless tousled head held up off the ground while Arnold tried to make out the man limping up towards him.

Tim was ten feet away when Holfinger sluggishly plunged one hand under his coat. Tim made two long steps and placed his foot over the forearm which was just outside Holfinger's coat. He bent, drew back the hand, and pried a little .41 calibre derringer from the clammy fingers. Holfinger slumped forward.

Tim knelt and rolled his victim over. Holfinger's face was dirty, his clothing torn and wrinkled. He looked straight up into Holbrook's face, conscious but hard hit. There was a spreading dark stain glistening over his shirtfront. The slug, Tim saw, had punctured Holfinger's lungs. He'd be filling up inside, his time growing shorter each passing moment.

"Damn you—Holbrook," the dying Texan whispered. "Damn you to hell!"

Tim tossed aside the derringer and said, "Take it easy, Arnold. It's over. One way or another it's all over."

". . . Lousy Brent . . . Didn't do it after all."

"Brent's dead, Arnold. The kid from Nevada killed him a while back."

"Grace's—brother. Brent told me—after he recognised that kid. How the hell—did he ever find Brent?"

"Rode the hate trail, Arnold. Kept at it. That's the trouble with gunfights, Arnold, even legal ones. All they ever seem to do is ensure other gunfights. But murder—that turns every man's hand against a bushwhacker like Brent."

"You—should've—been—a—preacher, Holbrook."

Tim watched Holfinger's lids turn heavy, his mouth turn stiff and clumsy at forming words. The tousled head weakly rolled from side to side. Holfinger's eyes grew very dark and misty. He roused himself once and said, "Holbrook—is this—the big one?"

" 'Fraid so, Arnold. Through the lights. You got any kin?"

"Kin? Hell no. Always been a—loner."

"What about the cattle, Arnold?"

". . . Don't care. Keep 'em if you want, Holbrook. . . . Don't care. What was that you said—'get killed over two lousy forty dollar steers' . . .?"

Tim nodded but did not reply. Holfinger's heavy lids fell half-way over the drying eyes, his jaw sagged, turning slack and still. Arnold Holfinger was dead.

Tim took out his sixgun unaware that there was no more firing. He reloaded while kneeling beside Arnold Holfinger, dropped the weapon back into its holster and looked up as several men came walking quietly up to halt and stare. It took a moment for him to believe that the lined, anciently wrinkled hard-set old face he was looking at belonged to old Sam Stubbs. Sam had a carbine in his hands. Around him were several other men who had not been present during the fight. One was Sam's other son, another was Charley Partridge, still another was the owner of the *Blue Mule* back in town.

Old Sam nudged Holfinger with his carbine barrel. "Dead?" he asked gruffly.

Tim nodded and pushed upright, winced when his injured leg shot a darting little pain up through him, and looked back beyond the men standing around Sam Stubbs. "He's dead," Tim said. "What happened back there?"

Charley Partridge said, "The survivors give up, Sheriff. But it'd still have ended the same way if we hadn't come up, I reckon. Of them nine fellers with Arnold, only three are still alive, and two of them are wounded."

Old Sam turned away from his long, bleak study of the dead Texan. "Your horses come runnin' into town. Ariel Spangler's critter had a streak of blood on the jockey-leather. The whole blessed town got in an up-

roar, Tim. There was some drovers come in this afternoon. They was runnin' around like chickens with
their heads lopped off, so I sort of took over. You
weren't around, otherwise I sure wouldn't have."

Joe Cane came up looking drained dry and dog tired.
He said, "Tim, we got Ariel and Jim in their wagon. I
come over to see if you want to ride back in the wagon
too."

Tim blinked. "Me? Why me, Joe?"

"Well, dammit all," exclaimed Cane, pointing. "You
been shot in the leg. Look at you, there's blood all
down your pants."

Tim looked. He looked as though he'd been butcher-
ing hogs. "Just looks bad," he mumbled. "How'd the
others come through, Joe?"

"Fair enough. I got nicked and Clay got a bad cut
on the cheek from where a slug hit the stock of his
rifle. But the best one's Jim. He got shot through the
ham." Cane smiled. "Now he can't stand up because
of his hurt hip, an' he can't sit down because of his
perforated ham. He's in a turrible fix."

"You?" Tim asked. "How bad's your leg."

"About like yours. Looks a sight worse'n it is. You
ready to head for town?"

Tim nodded, close to wryly smiling at Joe. "I've
been ready since early this morning."

Joe didn't grin back. He said, "Well, I reckon." Then
he looked at the others before saying, "Your buggy's
waitin' down there. The boys from town fetched back
our horses. We tied yours to the back of the buggy."

"What buggy, dammit? If my horse is here I'll
ride . . ."

"No, you won't, Tim," said Cane. "Miss Grace's in

the buggy waitin' an' we already tied the horse on behind. Come on; let's get going."

They all walked soberly back where the final scene of fighting had taken place. The dead had already been loaded and the injured, including uncomfortable Jim Sargent, were being helped into another wagon. There were cowboys and townsmen everywhere, some still holding carbines in their hands, some holding horses or talking together with Seldon or the Spanglers or Joe Cane.

Tim saw Grace seated in a top-buggy leaning forward. Speaking to her from one side was Bert. Their faces were animated, their voices pushing fast questions at each other and fast answers. When Tim walked over Bert saw him first.

He said, "Well, Sis, here's the ruggedest lawman I've ever run across." Bert grinned over at Holbrook. "If you're willin', Sheriff, I'd sure be proud to buy you the biggest steak in Bullhead, when we get back."

Tim nodded, wondering whether to ask Bert in front of his sister what had happened when he and Idaho Brent met some time back. "Sure," he said, leaning forward to get into the buggy with Grace. "Back in town we can do a lot of things."

Bert looked straight at Holbrook. He seemed to catch that innuendo, for he said, "He just wasn't fast enough, Sheriff. Maybe at back-shootin' he'd be faster, but like you said—unless I'd been practisin' he'd beat me. Well, I've done a lot of practisin' the past couple of years. An awful lot. Just about every day." Bert shook his head. "He wasn't even half fast enough."

Tim considered Bert's hard, bronzed, youthful face a moment, then he said, "Now what? You know, that's one of the hardest things about concentrating so long on just one objective, Bert. When you hit the end of the line and it's all finished—then you're sort of lost because you've been concentratin' on just one thing."

Bert stood a moment turning this over in his mind. Eventually he said, " 'Need a deputy sheriff in your county, Sheriff?"

Tim leaned back and grinned. "Might need one at that, Bert. We'll talk over that dollar steak you're goin' to buy me. Let's go, Grace. I need a bath, some clean clothes, a patch on my leg, a gallon of *Blue Mule* beer—then about twenty hours' sleep."

She shook the lines and wheeled the buggy away from the noise and ruin. As they started moving off two men walked past carrying Arnold Holfinger between them. Grace looked and painfully swallowed, but said nothing.

It was near nine o'clock. Ten hours since Sheriff Tim Holbrook had left town. Ten deadly, hot, menacing hours of not knowing from moment to moment whether he'd be alive at the end of them or not.

"Grace," he said, half-way back towards Bullhead, "you ever think of giving up the café?"

She didn't look at him. "I've thought of it, yes. What did you have in mind, Tim?"

"Gettin' married maybe, and startin' up in the cattle business." He swung his head. "Or maybe even start a saloon. I'm right partial to cool beer. In fact that's about all that's been in the back of my mind for the last five, six hours."

She said, "The trouble with you, Tim Holbrook, is that unless you're smiling I never know when you're kidding or not."

"You think I'm jokin'?"

"You'd better be. I'll marry you, which shouldn't

be any great surprise to anyone in the Bullhead country, but there'll be no saloon, with cool beer or without cool beer."

"All right," he said, watching the town lights moving ahead of them, looking warm and friendly. "Then you go on running the café and I'll just retire. Hang around the liverybarn and whittle, maybe."

"You are impossible," she said, thought a moment and gave him an affectionate little wan smile. "But when I don't know where you are, I worry."

"A good sign," he said, grinning back. "A very good sign. Anyway, we've got a sort of mutual responsibility. Your brother. Having gunmen around the house never did appeal to me, and if there's nothin' for him to return to Nevada for, then I reckon we'd best take him in hand, yank out the slack, straighten the kinks, and for gosh sake get him a haircut and a change of clothes. He looks like a sheepherder and by lord he even smells like one."

Grace said, "Whoa," to the horse, sat a moment with the lines slack, then purposefully looped them, turned and reached for Tim Holbrook with both hands. She kissed him flush on the lips, lay a long, soft moment against him, then, still without saying a word, got free, picked up the lines and flicked them. The horse started onward, the buggy creaked across rough ground, Bullhead's orange lights invitingly glistened, and beside her Tim Holbrook was sound asleep.

THE END